Accident Prone

Accident Prone

Michelle McGriff

URBAN
Renaissance

www.urbanbooks.net

Urban Books, LLC
78 East Industry Court
Deer Park, NY 11729

ISBN 13: 978-1-60162-323-2
ISBN 10: 1-60162-323-2

First Trade Paperback Printing November 2011
Printed in the United States of America

10 9 8 7 6 5 4 3 2 1

This is a work of fiction. Any references or similarities to actual events, real people, living, or dead, or to real locales are intended to give the novel a sense of reality. Any similarity in other names, characters, places, and incidents is entirely coincidental.

Distributed by Kensington Publishing Corp.
Submit Wholesale Orders to:
Kensington Publishing Corp.
C/O Penguin Group (USA) Inc.
Attention: Order Processing
405 Murray Hill Parkway
East Rutherford, NJ 07073-2316
Phone: 1-800-526-0275
Fax: 1-800-227-9604

Prologue

The rain was coming down in buckets.

So tonight of all times the weather forecast is right, she couldn't help but notice as she struggled along the slippery rocks.

Looking over her shoulder at the crashing waves, she could see all the bright lights and color in the distance. The worst thing would be for this to turn into a tragic accident. That would be all she needed.

The flames leapt high. Just hearing the bellows of the Coast Guard, as they called from portside, made her stomach tighten. Her hands slipped on some of the smoother rocks, but her foot had found solid ground as she continued to climb until the lights of the house came into view. All she could hope was that someone in the house would allow her to use the phone if need be, that her appearance would not be too frightening—and that they wouldn't ask too many questions. Questions would be impossible to answer right now, and the answers wouldn't be the ones they would want to hear.

Just then she saw the lights from a slowing oncoming car. What would normally seem like a strange time for someone to be on this road was in reality a successfully well-timed event. It was an elaborate part of this crazy plan she found herself involved in. It wasn't as well thought out as she had first imagined it to be, but sometimes you just had to go with what you had when you had it, she reasoned. Attempting to move a little faster, she tried to rush to the top of the cliff so as to flag the car down when it got closer.

"Shit," she spat as water drenched her face, blinding her. She needed to stop that car. She needed to catch her ride. Suddenly her foot slipped. "Shit!" she screamed as footing was lost and she felt herself sliding down the rugged side of the cliff. The front of her body hit everything hard on the way down. She didn't know what to grab on to or try to protect first. "I'm falling . . . oh God!" she cried out. This accident couldn't have been more real if she'd planned it this way.

Her head hit something hard. There was a sharp pain and then only a numb ache. Blackness came quickly.

Chapter 1

It was Sunday night; Lacy sat at her small but functional cherry wood desk. She sat on the edge of her simple but comfortable straight-backed chair, staring at the blank paper in her typewriter.

The quaint three-bedroom cottage had everything Lacy could ever need. Shellacked hard dark wood covered the floors, and the walls were papered with a paisley paper that must have resembled anybody's grandmother's walls. She liked it like that. She was eccentric and knew it, so why fight it.

Large bay windows on both the west and east ends of the house gave it an extraordinary amount of light during the day and an eerie, often unnerving, amount of transparency during the dusk and night hours. Perhaps if she closed the high-mounted drapes she would have more privacy, but then again who else lived on this cliff?

She had a crackling fire blazing in her fireplace. The Southwest décor added to the homey feel of her home. She had covered the largest area of the main living room's wood floors with a large, shaggy throw rug, which made the perfect bed for her two large dogs. The cage for Pete, her precocious talking parrot, hung at eye level for those moments when deep thought required a two-minute stare down with him. Yes, she was eclectic and eccentric, but it made life good from her point of view.

She made sure her kitchen was fully equipped with all the latest gadgets for cooking, though she had to admit she used hardly half of those utensils as she had yet to have any guests. She recalled the cashier totaling the hundreds of dollars spent on the heavy Alumacast pots and pans. Lacy had convinced herself that soon she would be the charming, trendy hostess of the housewarming party to end all housewarming parties. She imagined that winter evening, just two weeks after moving in, as she unpacked the trunk of her car, that she would soon fill her place with the sounds of old friends and warm wine and laughter. But now, after a year, it seemed like a foolish fantasy. It was already winter again, a day much resembling the one on which she moved in, and still only the sounds of her own voice and that of her bird, filled her empty home.

She remembered the moving guys, as she ran her hand over the sanded repair made to the edge of her desk. . . .

Yeah, she remembered the moving guys; the big guy was the worst.

"Hey, aren't you the voice?" he asked with a wide grin. Lacy nodded reluctantly, knowing what would surely come next. "Ya know this wouldna happened if you had a man around to move ya. You can't get rid of all of us." He grinned at her, his comment filled with innuendo. Again, her job and the reputation that had come with the cartoon character Amazon Queen Hynata the Manslayer had preceded her. The men snickered, chortled, and pointed, no doubt noting the lack of resemblance between the bulky cartoon woman and the string-bean, homely-looking woman standing before them, resembling, more than anything, a well-tanned, red-headed, freckle-faced Olive Oyl—with biggo, scary-looking blue eyes.

I'm not that bad, am I? she asked the large wall mirror. Shaking her head, she realized it didn't matter. It would never matter. Maybe those men saw a nobody, but inside Lacy knew that she was a somebody. She was a "shero."

"I'm Hynata, friggin' Queen of the Amazon," she said out loud with a chuckle, as she thought about the children's television show that appeared on television every day, right when the kids got home from school. Never appearing before the camera, she would live vicariously through the beautiful queen, as a guide, taking the children on the Amazon adventure.

Two years previously, she had started out just on the writing staff for the cartoon, and, by a fluke, ended up also becoming the voice-over for the Queen Hynata, who hated all men. To change the negative focus of the show, her hatred was translated into a hatred for "bad" men, who sought to destroy the Amazon Rainforest with their greed and neglect for the ecosystem. She was a character with the power to turn these "bad" men into salt whenever they did something bad to the earth. She didn't hate men at all, really; they just got on her nerves . . . Okay, so maybe there was a little love/hate thing going on, but she'd have gotten over it had one really, actually started "acting right" . . . ever.

After a few months of her successful run as the queen, the writing team had yet to find her equal, although the show's producers were building up to finding her a male counterpart who would, through love for her and Mother Earth, touch her heart with . . .

True love . . .

Bleech. She gasped, thinking about the possibilities.

Sensing her dethroning, Lacy began doing a lot of thinking about her future, and started writing in her spare time. Soon she was writing fiction, and, to her surprise, her first published effort as a writer landed her on *The New York Times* Bestseller list. It was funny how quickly all talks of adding to her fame subsided, but still it was only the cartoon that her bosses focused on.

"Not the book," she said, again in full voice, and smirked, thinking of the nonexistent book signings. The publisher felt it best not to destroy her air of mystery stimulated by her life as a cartoon voice-over.

"They must just think I'm ugly, that's all," she told her uninterested dogs. Lacy always came to that conclusion when unhappy or feeling rejected. But, in her opinion, the mirror didn't lie, and in her case beauty was definitely in the eyes of the beholder. Tall and lanky, less than shapely, with red kinky hair and blue eyes from her blended racial mix of Australian and Black always had her wondering just exactly where she fit in on the beauty scale.

"But at least I'm smart," she huffed, causing the female dog to look up at her.

The sudden ringing of her phone caused her to gasp loudly in a start, which sent her Australian shepherd/ black Labrador mixed dogs, Harriet and Oz, into a tizzy, ready to protect her from the enemy on the unseen side of the telephone. The loud-ringing house phone usually signaled a call from someone she didn't know. Those who knew her and wanted to find her and actually talk to her called her cell phone. The soft, tiny, seldom-ringing cellular phone, playing the catchy little jingle in her purse, was usually the only call she would take.

"Loner" was an understatement in describing Lacy's life. She'd always been alone, or at least felt that way. She'd come full circle in life. From standing behind the most popular girl in school to standing behind the camera that addressed millions after school hours and just recently on Saturday mornings too, she'd gone full circle only to end up feeling like an unnoticed, unappreciated weirdo outcast standalone.

As an only child, Lacy felt odd and displaced. By the time she got to high school she felt even worse about her life. She was not a member of the in crowd, and although she fought the hateful feelings she felt while watching them practice their cheers and hug up with the quarterbacks, she had to be honest—they had their appeal. Okay, so, yes, she was jealous. Maybe that was why she was drawn to Phoebe DuChamp, or maybe it was just to get close to her brother, Marcel. *Grrrrrroooowlllwow,* she purred at the memory of her high-school crush.

Marcel was the boy next door and the sister of the girl she loved to hate the most—Phoebe. In her more shameful moments, she would even admit to stalking Phoebe and accepting her pathetic attempts at friendship, and often humiliating abuses, just to get close to him. Many people assumed that she and Phoebe were the best of friends; only she and Phoebe knew the truth about that relationship. Or, better yet, maybe only she did. It was *way* one-sided. If they did anything together, it was purely due to Phoebe's need for a coat rack with legs, at least that's how Lacy felt about it.

Nonetheless, when Phoebe was bored, or especially during the winter months when things would slow to a crawl, they did things together and sometimes even resembled best buddies. One night, during a sleepover, they promised to will all their earthly possessions to each other. Lacy actually did put Phoebe in her will. She told her about it, too. It was after they'd graduated high school and Lacy started college. They continued to see each other occasionally when visiting their folks who still lived next door to each other. For Lacy, Phoebe still was just about her only 'friend'—use that term loosely. Besides, it wasn't as if she had anyone else to will things to if life went the way it was supposed to and she outlived her parents. *So why not?* she'd thought at the time as a broke and starving college student. *Why not will all my fortunes to Phoebe DuChamp?*

Lacy remembered that Phoebe seemed touched by the will. That's when Lacy knew that Phoebe really wasn't all that evil. She had a vulnerable side. She just wanted someone to love her, but that was conflicted with a more aggressive side, one that also knew how to take what she needed—even without permission—and that included love.

Phoebe just used her because she was there for the using. It wasn't Phoebe's fault, and she wasn't that bad of a person, she was just one of the "them" in Lacy's life. Lacy knew that Phoebe was on the side of all those who made her feel small. "Yeah, I was pretty small back then," Lacy continued thinking back at some of the most embarrassing moments in life. The phone rang the memories came. It was as if time stood still for a moment. eerie and surreal. The memories seemed to pass like hours, yet it was as if a flash in time. Like that night in the DuChamps' backyard.

Blame it on the thunder, blame it on Phoebe, but it all worked out. The girls from the cheerleading squad had a sleepover in the backyard of the DuChamps' house, and Phoebe had invited her over. During that autumn night, the weather took a freakish turn and lightning crossed the skies. Lacy was terrified. Everyone else showed no fear. It was more than obvious that no one wanted to be the first to run inside. But Lacy wasn't about to play chicken with the weather. It had won hands down, no competition with the "it" girls.

They weren't "it" to the thunder. She wasn't scared of much, but thunder and lightning were at the top of her short list. Often in their region there would be thunder and lightning but no rain. California could have some of the most fantastically beautiful autumn nights, and some of the scariest, weather-wise.

The girls, growing tired of her whimpering, sent her out of their tent into the darkness. "Go on home, ya big baby," one of the girls had said.

Lacy didn't look back to see who it was. She didn't really care. She was planning to head for home and the safety of her own bed. Lacy's trip was cut short by loud booms. Instead of crossing the fence line she dashed into the boys' tent, which held only Marcel and his friend Winston. Both boys had been assigned by Phoebe's parents to sleep out with them for protection . . . supposedly.

Lacy dashed into the tent and quickly into Marcel's sleeping bag. Although uninvited, Marcel didn't ask her to leave, but instead stared deep into her eyes. It was obvious he saw her fear, and instead of making her feel even more foolish, he wrapped his arms around her and held her.

"I'm so scared," she whispered into his chest.

"Don't be, Lace, it's just noise," he whispered back.

His voice was low and deep, rumbling with a comfort Lacy had never felt before but from that day forward would crave. Snuggling closer, she felt a strange thing rubbing against her thigh. She started to raise the sleeping bag flap to see what it was, but Marcel stopped her.

What happened next was natural, pure, and beautiful.

Lacy thought back to that night: the tent, the sleeping bag, the thunder, Marcel's best friend, Winston, snoring loudly in the bag not too far away. They were quiet as mice, nobody heard anything, but she felt everything.

Marcel was gentle. It was obvious it wasn't his first time. Maybe he assumed the same for her, but it wasn't true. Marcel was the first boy to venture between her thighs. She'd not even worn a tampon, so all the sensations he caused to come up were quite new. Sometimes Lacy thought back to how easily she allowed that to happen and how unaccountable she allowed Marcel to be afterward. "Pretty small of me," she mumbled, shaking her head at the sad memory.

Lacy sighed heavily at the memory. The next morning, Phoebe had gasped loudly after she busted into the tent while in a mad search for her. Lacy was mortified. Standing there as if frozen, Phoebe just stared as if she'd stolen something. Or maybe she was wondering what it had been like to have sex with her brother. She never asked, nor had she told the others; at least, it seemed as though she hadn't, as the others continued to see Lacy as the "can't get a guy" loser that she was.

Loser, she thought. *Can't get a guy,* she went on thinking, as her mind dripped on and quickly off of Marcel.

"But that was then. This is now. Now, I'm a success. I'm a biggo fabulous success and can't be daydreaming over some childhood crushes and stuff." She was being sarcastic, but who was there to hear it?

Nobody, she thought.

Lacy's ride to success had been far from fabulous, however. The trip came with frequent recurring nightmares, insomnia, headaches, and hives as fare. Her therapist suggested that a move near the water might relax her mind and spirit. Her physician concurred. Living there on the cliffs was indeed a stress-free lifestyle, though sometimes, as she lay in her king-sized netted canopy bed hugging her body pillow, she wondered if it had been worth it.

Her stress level had gone down tremendously since her move up to the cliffs of Half Moon Bay, California.

At least until tonight, she thought as her mind came back to the ringing phone.

"Hello, hello," Lacy answered. She was almost short of breath from the excitement brought on by the dogs' overreaction to the ring. Their barking had awakened Pete the bird, who was now cursing loudly, as was his normal vocabulary.

The telephone line was silent.

"Hello," Lacy repeated.

There was no sound from the other end. She hung up and glanced at the clock. *Wrong number at eleven P.M.? How frickin' rude,* she thought. *You'd think people would know who the hell they were calling at eleven P.M.*

The weather outside had taken a turn for the worse and the promised storm was coming in fast. Crashing winds against the rocks and the thunder could be heard in the distance. The waves crashed against the cliffs, sounding like an explosion. Lacy was terrified. She wondered now if this house truly had been the best of investments for lowering her stress.

The phone rang again. Lacy grabbed it quickly. The sound of the hard rain fell against the window in rhythm with the murmuring of the trees, groaning with the harsh bullying of the winds shoving against them.

"Hello!" she barked.

"Lacy?" The voice was soft and whimpering. "It's Phoebe . . . She's dead."

Lacy dropped the phone in shock. When she picked it up again, the line was dead. Immediately she called her parents. If indeed Phoebe DuChamp was dead, her parents would have heard it first from Phoebe's parents next door.

Chapter 2

What a reunion after all these years, Lacy thought as she watched lines of cars and limousines pulling into the cemetery. She could see so many familiar faces through the car windows as they passed. Many of the people she had gone to school with were here. Many of the DuChamps' relatives from out of town had arrived. Lacy recognized many from the years of living next door to the DuChamps. Lacy had even spotted her own parents' car parked with the others near the gate. She had known they were coming, but hadn't made plans to drive in with them. She'd not even been the one to tell them about Phoebe's death. By the time she'd called, they already knew. But, then again, they still lived next door to Phoebe's parents, Pia and Theloneous DuChamp.

The rain was heavy and it was hard to distinguish the drops of water from the falling tears on the faces of many. Pia and Theloneous climbed out of the back of one of the limousines as it pulled to a stop. Right after . . .

"Marcel," Lacy heard herself say in an undertone.

Lacy's heart jumped. She was a little surprised at the reaction in her chest. Could there still be that . . . something . . . there? Could there still be that something that always fought against the reasoning, the reasoning that told her that if he hadn't contacted her in nearly two years, chances were he really wasn't that into her?

Bad timing, Lacy; bad time for being reasonable, she told herself.

Lacy hadn't seen Marcel in a long time, but even with that, today he really didn't look like the Marcel she remembered. As he waved to the man handing out umbrellas, signaling him to shelter his parents, she could see his thick, dark hair was flat from the rain, his face was stony and cold, and the smooth Mediterranean complexion that he and Phoebe had shared was pale and lifeless. He walked slowly behind his parents, who were shielded from the rain by the large umbrella.

Suddenly, he looked around slightly as if looking for someone, and then only straight ahead. She had imagined that she had pulled at his heartstrings. She wanted to believe that, for surely he had pulled at hers.

Lacy didn't cry at the gravesite as the minister gave the eulogy. He was very to the point and covered Phoebe's life succinctly. It sounded almost as if he knew her.

Free spirited, loving, and kind was how he summed her up. Yes, that was Phoebe . . . Well, at least the Phoebe everyone wanted to remember. It was the Phoebe most people knew. The Phoebe Lacy knew, however, was catty, jealous, self-absorbed, self-destructive, angry, perhaps a bit cynical, and maybe just slightly on this side of darkness. It wasn't until she married Harold that Lacy would add pitiable to the list.

Looking around, Lacy spied Denise. Denise was part of Phoebe's in crowd. Denise was one of those girls who most other girls loved to hate. She was black, but managed to cross color lines, as she could blend in with any racial crowd she was a part of without giving in to ethnic stereotypes. Her parents made a good living and, therefore, Denise lived a middle-class suburban life. Maybe in another time she would have been called citified or uppity, but to the crowd that she was a part of in San Jose, California, she was just cute and crazy Denise.

She was a fiery black girl who swore no man could "tame" her. Eugene, who was eight years older than she, was a widowed banker with two small children. He was the manager of the bank where she had landed a summer job in her senior year. They married not too long after graduation, right after Phoebe's wedding. The last time Lacy had checked, Denise was a happy and very "tamed" wife and mother.

Lacy could say that she and Denise were friends, inasmuch as Denise always seemed too preoccupied with her own life or gossip mongering to be hateful to her. Sometimes she would join her and Phoebe for a lunch date when in the city.

Lunch dates had not happened in a long time, Lacy thought now, feeling the gnawing of regret. Maybe she was the reason for her own loneliness. Maybe it wasn't anybody's fault but her own. She wasn't there when, apparently, Phoebe needed her most. But, then again, as she looked around for Sonja, Sonja was another one who wasn't there for Phoebe when Phoebe needed her most . . . like today.

Perhaps, being a top model in France has its demands beyond friendship, Lacy thought. Lacy inwardly felt judgmental. She knew inside that Sonja had been a good friend to Phoebe—good enough to be maid of honor in the wedding. Maybe Sonja and Denise were Phoebe's real friends. *Who am I to judge them?*

Despite what Lacy felt to be a fraudulent or counterfeit high-school friendship, she continued after graduation what she and Phoebe shared. She was even in Phoebe's wedding, which came within the year immediately following high school. After that, Lacy started college and Phoebe started her life as Harold's wife.

At first Lacy thought friendship with Phoebe might help in her efforts to get something going with Marcel, but that was a wash when he left town and headed to the city to join the police force. He hardly ever came home, even for holidays. Lacy always wondered why, but never asked Phoebe, as her drama seemed to grow bigger than life. It was always about her. Phoebe would ask and Lacy would answer. Phoebe would need and Lacy would give. Phoebe would call and Lacy would come. Perhaps there was a level of trust there . . . or loyalty . . . *like that between master and pet, ya know,* but Phoebe began to confide in Lacy more and more. She began telling her about the abuses she was enduring at the hand of Harold Kitchener, her husband. Lacy didn't always know what to believe, but she would always listen. Soon, Lacy forgot about her infatuation with Marcel, and slowly formed something real with Phoebe . . . real enough anyway. It was real enough for her to realize suddenly that her friend was dead.

Lacy's attention was drawn back to the surreal scene playing out in front of her that day. She suddenly felt strange inside. There was something wrong there. Maybe it was because she was watching Harold. When he took the podium to speak and was overcome with grief, she was hit with monumental confusion. Lacy knew things about Harold and Phoebe's marriage. She knew things that she probably shouldn't. Lacy's thoughts scattered while watching Harold's tears pour freely from his sky blue eyes.

Harold was crying, and Marcel was not. But, then again, what was there to cry about? Phoebe wasn't even in that casket.

Phoebe's body had not been recovered from a boating accident that had occurred not too awfully far from where she lived in Half Moon Bay. An explosion like that left very few remains behind, according to the Coast Guard. So what was going into the ground was an empty shell.

Parts of Phoebe were cold, empty, and void of anything warm and loving. So in many ways it was poetic justice that her coffin was void of anything fleshly. She would have liked it that way anyway. She was vain where her looks were concerned, and would not have wanted anyone looking at her lifeless self without her being able to explain any flaws that may have been found by those who may have scrutinized.

Phoebe hated admitting to her flaws. But, thankfully, Lacy was fully flawed so it made it easy for Phoebe to ignore her own. Anyway, back to the casket; it held precious things—a few photos, some jewels, and a letter from her parents telling her how much they loved her. So what was to cry over, a few trinkets?

Nothing that afternoon seemed in sync, or even real for that matter, nothing at all. The entire time since Lacy had gotten the call she'd been forced, it seemed, into a mental state of flashback. Everything seemed beyond surreal. *But, then again, I'm a frickin' cartoon for crying out loud. What do I know from real?* she thought as she moved through the crowd of people who had gathered this day to pay their respects.

Chapter 3

Heading to her car, Lacy was ready to follow the long row of slow-moving cars through the busy streets of South San Francisco to the Grange Hall where Phoebe's parents would host the repast. She noticed her own parents peeling off possibly heading toward home. She wanted to follow them, but felt the uncontrollable draw of the crowd. She'd not been to her parents' in a few weeks and missed them. During the gravesite funeral, she watched them. They were growing old. But, then again, today that didn't seem to matter. Burying someone as young as Phoebe made her parents' ages seem inconsequential.

As they piled into the Grange Hall, after sliding a glass of wine from the serving table, Lacy saw Denise in the crowd. Her face was buried in the lapel of her husband, Eugene. He was a large man, and Lacy could almost feel the comfort that Denise seemed to be feeling from just his heavy arm around her. She instantly felt cold and empty and lonely.

Maybe I am grieving. Maybe I do care. I do miss her. I do. Lacy took a large gulp from a second glass of wine.

Lacy thought now about Sonja. She had been the first to take a giant step into success. It had been her dream to be a model. Being nearly six feet tall in stocking feet, she would often say to the girls with true sincerity, "What other dream could I have? Women's basketball?" That modeling dream became a reality just months before graduation when her family moved to France. She'd come back for Phoebe's wedding to Harold.

Odd, how that day was more important than this day here. *Maybe because black was never your best color.* Lacy knew her thoughts were getting just plain out there.

Sonja wasn't that bad. She was just . . . fake, mean, hateful, and bitchy. Okay, so she was that bad. She was jealous of Phoebe, only Phoebe couldn't see past Sonja's beauty. It had to be fantastic having such a beautiful friend.

With Phoebe, Lacy sort of understood the draw. Phoebe had long raven black hair and dark, soulful eyes. Her lips were pouty, yet innocent—until she spoke. She cursed like a sailor without a port. Lacy smiled thinking about Phoebe's vocabulary.

Nonetheless, guys got past that. Many only to second base—quickly. Phoebe enjoyed sex and talked about it all the time. Sonja never spoke about it, although it was rumored she was competing with Phoebe for "best laid slut." Lacy had to figure Sonja was winning, as she didn't have a problem following up after Phoebe in addition to her own captures, which had to double her numbers in the end. Between the two of them, Phoebe and Sonja, they had the entire male population laid up, so to speak—*well, most of it.*

Lacy shook her head at her hateful thoughts, while setting her second empty glass down on the passing tray and moving away from it with a third glass of wine in her hand. This day was wearing her out emotionally. All the mixed feelings were just too much. Here she was, at a funeral for a woman who she felt so forced into liking . . . loving . . . sharing a big chunk of her life with. Toxic though it was, Phoebe had become the sister she never had. She wished she'd had a chance to tell her. Maybe she'd tell Marcel. Marcel was as close as she was gonna get to Phoebe ever again. But, then again, her love for Phoebe always spilled over onto Marcel, as Phoebe always seemed too busy to soak it all up.

Looking around, noting Harold, Lacy saw that he stood beside a woman who Lacy only sort of recognized. Only later did she find out the woman was his girlfriend. Perhaps it was just her lightly provincial and sarcastic ways, but that struck Lacy immediately as odd and bordering on bad form—*Sheesh, Harold, your current wife isn't even cold in the ground yet*—but this woman also went to their same school. She was a freshman when they were seniors. So if Harold had given her half a glance back then, she was a minor when he turned eighteen.

Yuck . . .

"*Buon appetito,*" Theo DuChamp announced loudly over the crowd, bringing Lacy's attention back to the moment she was in. He had a glass of wine in hand, and looked about halfway to being smashed. When had he started drinking, who would know, but no one seemed to mind his slurring words as the occasion certainly permitted. His eyes were wet with tears and his nose red from grief and inebriation. It was hard for Lacy to watch him, as he had always appeared to her to be a sober, hardworking, and gentle man. It was difficult to see him clearly forcing a smile to his face. Surely he had to be pretending to handle today's events with the same ease as he no doubt handled everyday life. Lacy remembered how Phoebe had been his heart. *Daddy's little girl.*

Lacy glanced around for her own father. To be truthful, she hadn't noticed if her parents had come at all.

She took them for granted. She really did. She felt as if they would be around forever. Glancing back at Theo DuChamp, she thought, *nobody does, though.*

Lacy moved through the crowd to the table where she found Denise sitting alone, eating. Eugene was off talking among the people there. *He seems as if he is a great schmoozer,* Lacy noticed. "Too bad Sonja isn't here. Was she called?" Lacy asked as she sat across from her at the small bistro table.

"Called? She's the one who called me," Denise answered quickly.

"You're kidding! I wonder who—" Lacy began, only to be interrupted by Harold joining their table. He was still being accompanied by the woman who, Lacy was about to find out, was his girlfriend. She was a thin, dark-haired woman. If you glanced at her quickly you would almost think she was Phoebe.

"Hello, girls," Harold said. Lacy noticed how the grief was now missing in his voice.

Harold was an arrogant ass as far as Lacy was concerned, but today she almost felt sorry for him. She would have if she'd never found out that the woman was his girlfriend.

"Oh, Harold, I'm so sorry. We are all just torn apart," Denise said, beginning to cry. She covered her face with her hands. Lacy was taken aback at the speed at which her tears came.

Grief does that to some people, Lacy reasoned, sipping her wine a little slower now, feeling it warming her chest. The emotional climate of this room was starting to get to her. It was hard to take. She was ready to leave.

"This is Victoria," Harold introduced. "Adam Stillberg's sister," he went on. Lacy thought she might also know the name Adam Stillberg. It was said to her as if she should.

Victoria's eyes darted away as she avoided eye contact with Lacy. She was looking uncomfortably over her shoulder and all around the room. Lacy felt bad for her in a way; it was clear she didn't feel as though she fit in. At this point Lacy didn't know she was Harold's girlfriend, but only this Adam what-his-name's sister. *Whoever the hell Adam is,* Lacy thought now, realizing how hazy her thoughts were becoming. She was feeling her wine a little. It had to be affecting her mind, for surely Harold appeared as if he was undressing her with his eyes again and again . . . fast, slow . . . and then again, this time with a nasty smile following the act. Lacy shook the thoughts from her head.

"Neee Ceeeeee, you're breaking my heart," Harold said then to Denise, bringing Lacy's attention back to what had to be reality. Harold was holding his chest in a dramatic gesture while leaning over and kissing Denise's forehead. She nodded without removing her hands from her face.

"It was a horrible accident," Denise said, her words muffled behind her hands as she sobbed. "I know you and your girlfriend are all busted up."

Harold began looking around as if wanting escape from the drama forming there at the table. "Oh, it's Phoebe's grandmother. I have to go talk to her," he said, spying Grandma DuChamp across the hall. Tugging at Victoria's arm, he pulled her along as he quickly fled the scene.

Girlfriend? Lacy's eyes bugged open with shock. *How crude can one person be? What about Phoebe? What is going on?* Turning back to Denise, Lacy saw her face was as dry as a bone. Lacy then turned to see if Harold had indeed gone in the direction of Grandma DuChamp. He was nowhere in sight.

"Lying dog," Denise muttered.

"What is going on?" Lacy asked.

"Did you see that bitch? Did you see her?"

Lacy turned to look. Denise snapped her finger to get Lacy's attention back in her direction. "Don't look . . . Just like . . . Look. Yeah, her? The bitch with Harold."

"Yeah."

"That's his lawyer's sister. Harold is banging his lawyer's sister." Lacy turned to look again, only to have Denise grab her cheeks and turn her face back. "That bitch is his lawyer's sister. Don't you think that's odd? And Adam Stillberg is his lawyer. Don't you think that's odd?"

"Harold having a lawyer or a mistress or . . . ?" Lacy asked between tightly squeezed cheeks.

Denise's eyes crossed. "Stay with me here." She shook her head and released Lacy's face. Lacy rubbed her reddening cheeks. "Harold's mistress being the lawyer's sister and the fact that they went to our school is just freaky, but then of course Phoebe probably slept with the guy, but I think that's really wild but not as wild of course as the insurance policy."

"Insurance policy?"

"Oh yeah, the insurance policy. It's a biggie," Denise said, taking a draw from her champagne flute.

"How big? No, wait, do I want to know?"

"Really big."

"How does someone like Phoebe—a housewife," Lacy interjected quickly so as not to sound as if putting Phoebe down in any way, "end up with a 'biggie' for an insurance policy?"

"Oh, I guess you didn't know. Perhaps y'all wasn't besties like you thought," Denise said, adding a sarcastic know-it-all smirk. She wasn't really a jealous person, just bitchy when she wanted to be. Actually,

Lacy wasn't sure how she truly felt about Denise. She liked her—but didn't. But, then again . . . did. What was there not to like? She was spirited and always full of information.

"We were friends—enough." Lacy sighed and rubbed her head. She thought back to her last few visits with Phoebe. She tried to remember if anything stood out. Sure, Phoebe said she had something to tell her, but didn't spill anything important on the visit. Hell, she didn't even spill that Harold was having an affair, which was apparently obvious—*I mean, Denise knows about it!* Lacy's mind added. She hoped her thoughts didn't show on her face.

"Let's just say her movie career had taken off."

"Movies? Phoebe wasn't a movie star."

"Look, you're not the only famous person around."

"I'm not famous."

"Whatever. Phoebe always felt you were. She was jealous of you, ya know."

"What? How do you know all this stuff?"

"I just do, but, most importantly, I know there's gonna be some serious drama jumpin' off when that insurance policy pays off."

"Why?"

"Because I heard that Phoebe didn't leave the money to Harold. I heard she left it to her lover."

"Lover? Phoebe didn't have a lover. She would have told me she had a lover," Lacy argued. "Now that I know."

Denise took another long draw from the flute. "I bet you do."

"Okay, so I don't know." Lacy looked over her shoulder self-consciously. "Tell me who Phoebe's lover is. Do you know? Is he here?"

"Stop playin', of course I know. You do too, so stop playin' around," Denise whispered before taking another, quicker, sip of champagne. Lacy's face must have said it all as Denise's eyes widened and she choked on her sip. "Oh my God, you don't know."

Lacy shrugged stupidly.

"You are her beneficiary," Denise then said.

Lacy covered her mouth in shock. "Noooo," she gasped. "That can't be right. I mean we weren't . . . You said lover . . . We weren't . . ."

"With the double indemnity clause that policy is worth millions—sweetheart." Denise winked at her. "I knew something was fishy between you two. I mean, why would she be involved with someone like you?"

"Thanks."

"Seriously. You have never fit in. Frankly, I don't see what she saw in you as a girlfriend. Maybe someone sexy like me, sure, but then again . . ." Denise winked teasingly. "Queen Hynata . . ."

"Nooooo," Lacy yelped, although her tone was quiet. "You got it all wrong. I'm strictly dickly. You got it all wrong. We were just friends."

"No worries. I believe you." Denise laughed.

"Really. I'm not." Lacy's head swayed heavily back and forth. She was feeling the wine big time. "We were not lovers."

"I'm playin', but seriously, you're gonna need a friend when Harold gets through with your ass. He's gonna fight for that money you know."

"I don't want it. I don't . . . I don't need it. I . . . think you're wrong. You said she left it to a lover and that's not me. So she didn't leave it to me."

"Whatever. Maybe you didn't know she loved you. Doesn't matter. You getting paid for that love now."

Chapter 4

The bay breeze was cold. *It blows the rain every whichadamn way, and is messy, too,* Boyd complained to himself. Considering the weather report hadn't predicted a day like this, it was pretty damn inconvenient. She'd said it was going to be sunny. The windblown, soaked, thin-jacket-wearing, body-hugging tourists outside his downtown loft had verified that fact.

The weathergirl on the local TV station had not been accurate for a day since she first appeared on TV. She was a wash. *If you pardon my pun.* He chuckled under his breath at his own little joke. But seriously people still loved her. Boyd Jameson considered himself an observant man, and that was what he had observed. He finished up his burger and tossed his wrapper. It missed the trash. He started to put it in the receptacle, but just then the beautiful redhead with the striking blue eyes drew his attention back.

"So, you're telling me that just one drop of this can kill how many people?" she asked.

"As many as you want. It like . . . assimilates and dissipates and . . ." he attempted to explain.

"Okay, okay, I don't need a vocabulary lesson. I just wanted to know how many people this could kill at one time with just this little bit. I guess I expected to need more."

"If you plan to take out an army. I mean it's basically untraceable. But, then again, you aren't trying to do that, right? You aren't trying to . . . kill anyone . . . right?" He stammered just a little bit now. He sort of wondered about her desire to get her hands on such a lethal thing as this. But money had clouded his reasoning, until now. Now he was getting a little nervous, he had to admit.

"How much money do I owe you?" she cut in.

"Oh, you like getting to the point, huh? I guess with the position you're in, you must have a lot to lose wasting time, huh? Uh, before we make this transaction, tell me again what you plan to do with it."

"Look, you are getting on my last nerves beleaguering me with all this meandering of business."

"Beleaguering," Boyd repeated, impressed with the new vocabulary word he planned to use as soon as this transaction was over. He liked words. Looking around, he hoped the woman didn't realize he was trying to put the new word into another sentence. "If you do it right, it could look like an accident. I mean, for instance, if you put it in an air conditioning duct, it could blow out and slowly kill somebody without even forensics being the wiser. It would just look like natural causes. I mean, unless they really looked close." Boyd then said before bursting into laughter, exposing a mouthful of bad teeth. They were ugly enough to make a person flinch. He knew this. "But, then again, there are very few accidents that involve mercury these days, so they may not look at all."

"An accident is just what I had in mind," she said before suddenly whipping out a .22 and shoving it into his gut. "Put some of this on your tongue," she ordered, holding out a small vial toward him.

"Oh, hell nah!" he exploded. "I don't know what that shit really is."

The gun cocked. "Put some on your tongue," she ordered, her voice growling. "Put enough," she said, implying a lethal dose, "to make it look like an accident."

She was not kidding. Boyd knew that. She wanted him to kill himself with whatever she'd brought in that vial. It was either that or she was going to do something messy with that gun. He looked at the small vial and then again at her and then again at the gun. "Why?" he asked.

"Here's why. You're a gottdamned fuckin' loser and snitch. That's the shit you fuckin' do. I heard about you. You sell shit and then you go to the cops and tell. I can't have you going to the fuckin' cops about our little fuckin' transaction at a later time."

"I wouldn't fuckin' do that! I'm the one selling you this illegal shit. So I'm not gonna put your illegal fuckin' shit in my mouth. I know it's illegal because you trying to get me to take it." Now they were using words he easily understood.

"Look, you can fuckin' do it, or die writhing in pain on the ground after I put a bullet in your neck. I'll shoot you without even blinking. I'm a damn good shot. I will make sure to miss everything vital so that you don't die right away. And, trust me, I will shoot you without hesitation, right out here where nobody is even thinking about dropping by for a really long time. You could die slow, Boyd. Real slow."

"Oh my fuckin' God—"

"Yeah! That's what I'm talkin' about." She nodded. "And, for your information, what I have isn't illegal. Okay, before you die, tell me again. Now, you said this is untraceable and painless, right? I wouldn't want anybody to have pain." The gun held steady and Boyd realized he had limited choices about what to do with the rest of his life, which probably only had about ten more minutes to it. "Like, for instance, this here," she held up the vial. "You're gonna die right away and without any pain."

"Shit," he sighed, taking the vial from her hand.

Maybe he wouldn't die immediately. Maybe he wouldn't die painlessly. What a time to be wondering shit.

Feeling the sting as the small amount of liquid ravished the soft tissue of his tongue, Boyd cried out. Grabbing his throat, he dropped to his knees as the heat increased. His eyes widened and burned as if on fire. His hand jerked outward, reaching for the woman who jumped back from his grasp as he fell forward, gasping for air.

"Oh, mah bad, I guess you were wrong about the pain thing. Well, I sure hoped you aren't. I have a lot of money riding on this little bottle," she said, looking around while holding up the vial she had purchased from Boyd. It only took a minute or two longer of Boyd jerking and, every so often, wriggling before finally, with eyes open and mouth agape, Boyd Jamison died.

The woman reached the car parked in the inconspicuous location. Climbing in, she pulled off her red wig.

"What took you so long?" her partner asked.

"Needed exact change," the woman laughed wickedly.

Chapter 5

The rain had paused for a moment, just long enough for Lacy to make a quick run for her car. She hurried inside and started the engine for the heater. Rain always made her feel cold although it really was sort of a warm rain today.

Her mind was spinning. "Beneficiary? Oh my God," she heard herself saying aloud. "Lover?" she heard herself ask even louder. "Denise has to be wrong." Reaching for the radio, she noticed her hands shaking. She'd had too much to drink but, still, she had to get home. Somehow she had to get home. She had to get home, get in the bed, and cover up her head until she could no longer hear Denise's voice or see her face smirking at her as if to say, "Shame on y'all, you naughty little lesbians."

How could Phoebe tell people that lie? What is going on? Looking over her left shoulder toward the parked cars lining the street, she thought about her parents. Maybe they would show up to this shindig later and she'd just jump in their car. She was being hopeful. Her daddy would be a great one to see right now. He would know what to do. He would know what she should think.

Suddenly there was a knock on the passenger window. She jumped in a start. It was Marcel. Her heart began to pound like crazy. That only made her head spin more. She wasn't sure if it was from the scare or her excitement to see him. She hesitated too long, and he tapped on the window again.

"Oh . . . oh, yeah," she stammered, fumbling with the button until the right window finally lowered.

"Nice car." He smiled, admiring the leather seats that matched the exterior color of her Mercedes: powder blue.

Heat rushed to her face. Was she embarrassed over the extravagance of her car choice or the thoughts running through her mind? Had Marcel heard the rumor? The color of the car wasn't her choice really. Her boss felt she needed an image improvement to go along with the undercover fame of being Hynata, Queen of the "man haters." She'd straightened her bushy mop of wild, curly hair, had acrylic nails applied, added a few shorter skirts to her wardrobe, and, why not, a new car to finish off the look. Good-bye, Ford Taurus. Hello, Mercedes. Phoebe had said it was a good choice.

Her father had picked it out. She would smile every time, remembering the day they went together to get it. He was so proud of her that day. She had picked him up and they drove all the way to Chico to buy it. He had fought her on the color and felt she should go with red. "Too much, Daddy, too much," she had said, pointing to her red tresses that lopped loose around her shoulders. He then laughed in agreement.

"I, uh, didn't remember until now that I didn't bring my car, and, well, there's nobody here I'd rather have take me home than an old friend of Phoebe's," he said before breaking into that sexy little crooked smile of his. His voice, too, was a turn-on, deep and sultry as always. Lacy fell in love all over again. It must have shown, as Marcel walked around to the driver side of the car.

Without a second thought, she unlocked the door and slid from out of the driver seat into the passenger side while Marcel got in. "Hope none of the guys see me drivin' this baby. With my salary, they'll think I'm on the take." He chuckled.

Lacy laughed too, a little bit too loud. She was still out of sorts and now a little nervous on top of it. Of course, and her face grew hot.

He patted her leg. She stared at his hand as it seemed to linger there on her thigh. "It's all right, Lace, really," he said softly. She didn't know what he meant by that, but right now she didn't care. She just wanted to be with him. Her secret hero, he would take away her fear today, not of the thunder, not even of her own mortality, but a fear she didn't fully understand. The thought of what Denise had told her had started to settle a bit and as it crossed her mind, it brought fear with it.

Marcel had always called her Lace instead of Lacy. He was the only person who did. She hadn't heard it in such a long time and immediately she felt good. All the time since she'd last seen him faded away. It was as if it had been two weeks ago, instead of two years.

According to Phoebe, Marcel had just gotten too busy for family and friends. He became very private with his life, shutting everyone familiar out. At first it seemed as though Phoebe didn't care much, but as time passed she seemed more personally dejected by his obvious absence from family functions. Marcel hated Harold but, still, *who didn't?* Lacy's mind interjected. Nonetheless, Lacy couldn't believe Marcel had let his bad feelings for Harold come between him and his sister. Maybe Phoebe had told him about the two of them? "Oh my God," Lacy sighed aloud under her breath. She then looked over at Marcel to see if he heard her. Maybe Marcel believed the rumor! "Oh my

God," she sighed again. It wasn't as if she'd ever come out with her true feelings for him. It wasn't as if he knew, right? He would have believed anything.

When she realized she loved him, she was planning to go through Phoebe to get to him. She'd learned from watching those girls use people to get what they wanted, but the more she tried to use Phoebe, the more time she spent with her, until eventually Lacy never could seem to fit her feelings for Marcel into her and Phoebe's friendship. Soon Marcel had taken a back seat to her intentions for her and Phoebe's friendship. Maybe that was why it had become too easy for him to disappear from view. She always had intentions of getting back to him, but it just never worked out. She could never get around Phoebe. Soon she just gave up and gave in to what she and Phoebe had. Perhaps it was unhealthy, maybe even toxic, but it was what it was. Apparently she didn't know what it was, as Denise clearly exposed the gaps.

She was thinking way too hard now, realizing then that she was staring at the side of Marcel's head as he fiddled with her radio. He looked over at her now. In his eyes she could see a little bit of Phoebe still there. No matter what, Phoebe was always going to be between her and Marcel. Lacy leaned her head back and closed her eyes.

Chapter 6

The sound of thunder crashing jolted Lacy from her deep sleep. She sprung up in the bed. Her bed. She could hear the toilet flush in the hall bathroom. "Who . . . ?" she started to ask but caught her own voice. She knew. Looking at her naked body under her covers, she knew. "Marcel?" she called out softly. But he didn't answer. She tapped the bottom of the lamp that sat on the nightstand.

Her room was neatly furnished. Most writers she knew or heard about had such messy bedrooms, but not her. She did all her creating in the office, where creativity belonged. She'd not been creative in her bedroom in ages—in any kind of way. Everything in the room had a logical order and purpose. There were no frilly doilies, or pretty ceramic jars that served no logical purpose but to sit on the bureau. Only wild, colorful pillows filled her bed and she believed there was a totally logical reason for them being there—her mother had made them being the biggest one.

There was a place for everything and everything had a place. No dirty socks in the corner or underwear on the floor. There were no manly messes here . . . *Oh yeah, that wasn't me doing that. That was my long-time-over lover, Nyles. I almost forgot about him,* she lied to herself—again.

So many times she had been made to realize that Nyles really had been the slob her mother said he was. She thought the way he lived was normal for men.

Nyles was the first sort of real relationship Lacy had ever had. She was with him for about a year, after accepting that Marcel was not going to wake up and realize she was the only woman for him. After that night in the backyard he'd acted as if what had gone on between them had never happened. Eventually she too tried to believe it hadn't. Surely it had been an unplanned event in her life. Maybe if she tried hard enough she would make it an undone event in her universe. Marcel had seemed to make it that way.

Finishing high school and all that came with that traumatic experience, she watched as her classmates and all the popular girls got married and moved on, including Phoebe. Lacy, on the other hand, went off to college.

During college she met Nyles. He was a Navy man stationed there in the city. After just about six months of living together in her small apartment there in Daly City, she thought they would marry, but Nyles felt it would be inconvenient, especially since he already had a wife in Florida. Lacy was humiliated and quit school. Moving home to San Jose, back to her old room in her parents' house, next door to the DuChamps, she tried to recover. Nonetheless, at the first holiday, during a dinner party at her parents' house, Lacy made the mistake of telling Phoebe about what had happened with Nyles, only to be further mortified when Phoebe told Marcel all about it. That settled it, and as soon as she had the next opportunity to get back into San Francisco University and away from San Jose where they all grew up, she took it.

After Nyles, short of a nice overnight hotel date, she made up her mind to never have a man in her home or get serious about one again.

You're waiting for Marcel, she would tell her mirrored reflection, only to deny it by sticking out her tongue at herself.

But it was true, and she felt wasted. Life waiting for Marcel had turned into a big, fat waste.

Just then she heard the water running in the hall bathroom. Her heart jumped. She sat still for a moment, regrouping, before throwing back the covers and grabbing her robe off her bedroom door hanger. She slowly opened the bedroom door and padded lightly into the hall. Peeking around the wall into the living room, she saw him. There on the sofa. Marcel. He was without his shirt, and only wearing his boxer briefs . . . navy blue. He wrestled a moment with the small throw that he'd apparently kicked off and then tried to recover with, before settling in and closing his eyes. Clearly being resourceful, he'd apparently started a fire earlier in the fireplace, as the low-burning embers crackled in its slow death.

Outside her bay window, she could see that dawn was forcing its way through the thick clouds. She crept closer to him. She wanted to get a good look as the fire's reflection danced off his dark hair. The lines etched in his beautiful face gave him the expression of serious thought. Although his eyes were closed, a wrinkle formed between them. His mouth, his full lips, turned wickedly upward at one end, and gave the appearance of a half smile. His bare shoulders were muscular; sure, maybe he wasn't Abercrombie & Fitch, but he was surely *GQ*—and beautiful. Fanning at the air and squirming into a comfortable position, his entire chest became exposed. She stared as if watching a miracle unfolding. It was truly one of those mornings that would etch itself in her memory . . . along with the pounding pain that suddenly surged through her head. She groaned loudly.

Marcel's eyes opened wide and he jerked in a startle. "Sorry. I forgot that you guys really do sleep with one eye open," she whispered, holding out her hand to stop him from jumping up and shooting her or something else crazy.

"And with my gun." He smiled, returning to a sleepy-eyed state and readjusting his posture to a more up-right position against the arm of the short sofa. "Why are you up?" he looked at his watch. "It's six in the morning."

"Oh, uh, the noise," she confessed. "I don't like the thunder." She smiled sheepishly. She said it as if he didn't remember.

"Oh that's right. It always did scare you," he said, showing her he did indeed remember. "Jeez, Lace, it's just noise." His voice lowered to an almost suggestive tone . . . that is, if Lacy let her imagination go there. Sliding to one side on the short sofa he flopped back the small but heavy throw. It was like déjà vu and Lacy's knees felt instantly weak. To keep them from buckling, she climbed in, snuggling close and spreading the blanket throw over the two of them.

Lacy didn't want to spoil the moment by asking if he wanted to go get in the bed with her. Besides, that would be too much like really sleeping together and they hadn't even had their first real date. This was just another accidental encounter. Sort of like when they slept together the first time. . . .

It was a secret that the three of them, Lacy, Marcel, and Phoebe, who all but seemed in the room now, shared. Lacy had often wondered if he had forgotten that night or if he had too thought about it. Had it sometimes caused him to lose sleep, to yearn and burn deep inside, beyond the flesh and to the core? Like now, as he slept so close to her on that tiny sofa, did he want it as bad as she did?

Morning came on in and the smell of fresh-brewed coffee filled her nostrils as she stretched now. Marcel was off the sofa. . . .

Gone? Of course not! Who would be making the coffee, dumb-dumb? she asked and then answered herself.

Slowly throwing off the small, heavy crocheted afghan blanket throw that her mother made, she stood and stretched before heading into her kitchen. Stepping in the bright, spacious kitchen, she noticed her coffee pot ending its brew without supervision. Two plates were out on the bistro table she rarely used—as she commonly ate on the run. Smiling, she began to wonder what all this meant. Considering Marcel was nowhere around, it was hard to imagine it meant a step toward something like dating or, an even wilder thought, cohabitation. She laughed out loud at her crazy mind before, suddenly, she realized her dogs were gone.

"I hate you," Pete yelped. It was obvious to her; Pete probably knew where they were. *Maybe he'll tell me,* she thought before realizing how crazy that would be.

Turning, she ran out to the living room where his cage hung uncovered. She never left his cage uncovered. *Marcel's curiosity must have gotten the best of him,* she thought. "And I'm sure you were as rude as ever, you bastard," she said to Pete.

"You bastard," Pete repeated, as was their common exchange.

Just then her door opened and Marcel entered with a small pink box. He wore the suit he'd had on the night before at the funeral only without the jacket. The normally more suspicious and ready-to-bite-somebody-in-a-heartbeat dogs rushed in past him.

Phoebe had given Lacy the dogs as pups. It was a couple of years ago. She had bought the dogs and wanted to raise them, but Harold said no. She was devastated and called Lacy in a life or death panic. Lacy was too glad to take them off her hands. Phoebe had been the only person the dogs would allow in the house without a total hostile investigation taking place . . . barking, snarling . . . the works.

And now Marcel.

She ran her hands through the curly mop on her head as Marcel patted Oz on the head and followed him into the kitchen.

"You'd think that a bakery would have been closer. No, actually I would have thought you would have had donuts in this place. Big enough kitchen . . . Nothing in it," he commented casually.

"Well, there's only me, and, well . . ." Lacy stammered, following them.

"You bastard," Pete squawked. "I hate you."

Marcel turned and glared at the bird.

"I'm so sorry," Lacy apologized.

"Why, he's just speaking his mind and, well, he's probably right."

"Uhhh, no, no, he's not . . . He's not," Lacy stammered.

Marcel opened the box after washing his hands, and loaded maple bars onto the small plates. "Phoebe's favorites, but then again . . . you know that, right?"

"No, yeah, uh . . . Marcel, I . . . uh," Lacy stumbled. "About last night—"

"Nothing happened last night, Lace."

"But I woke up naked and—"

"Nothing happened last night." He smiled. She noticed then the slight twinkle in his eye, but ignored it.

"I mean, I'm sure it didn't," she said quickly, tightening the belt of her robe and grabbing a seat at the small table. "I'm sure I would have remembered it. I mean, of course I would have. I've waited forever for it, so I surely would have . . ." She stopped herself.

The heat from her words shot across her face and she was sure it was now as red as her hair. Marcel said nothing as he joined her at the table, carrying the coffee carafe.

"So, how has life been treating you up on this biggo hill?" he asked.

Lacy cleared her throat, nervously tucking her hair's loose curls behind her ear. Her robe was large and the sleeves flopped over her hands. "I have a vacation coming up so . . ."

"And that means . . . ?"

"I'll be seeing your folks in a few weeks when I go to visit my folks while I'm on vacation," she said—instead.

Instead of the words that had hung on the tip of her tongue for as long as she could remember—those four little words. *I love you, Marcel,* she thought.

"Good," he answered. "Vacations never come for me. I'm not sure I'd even know what to do on vacation. What, go see my parents? That would be awkward as hell. After all this time and now with . . . with . . ."

"Now with Phoebe gone?"

"Yeah. I mean, it's all too weird and frankly . . ." Marcel abruptly stopped speaking. He took a big bite from the donut and looked at the window.

"Frankly what?"

"You bastard," Pete squawked.

"Oh my God," Lacy said. She jumped to her feet and rushed out to the living room to cover Pete's cage. When she turned to head back into the kitchen, Marcel was standing behind her. She jumped slightly at his presence.

"Lace, do you believe in predestination?"

"No," she answered quickly. She wasn't sure if she did, but she wanted to sound sensible and altogether serious.

"So you think everything is just happenstance or that we all just bumble through life having one accidental life experience after another."

"Well no, but—"

He kissed her. "Like, oops, I just kissed you and . . ." he said before removing her robe from her shoulders. He touched her breasts, causing her nipples to stand tall and hard. Lifting one, he suckled it. "Oops," he said again, sexier this time. Lacy could not keep kitty's instantaneous purr from escaping her lips. Their eyes met.

Scooping her up in his arms he carried her to her bedroom. Undressing quickly, Marcel then cleared her bed of the large pillows that filled the side she left empty. Lacy stood, watching him make a mess on what was once her tidy floor.

A large canopy bed with Arabian sheers draping it gave the bed a fantasy look, which she only now appreciated to the fullest. Turning to her, he slid her robe completely from her and looked her naked body over.

"You can think whatever, Lace, but this is destiny right here," he said, sounding proud and positive that what he was saying was truth. Lacy could do nothing more than moan at the thought of what it would be like . . . again.

He tossed her onto the bed and all but dove into her as if jumping into a wading pool. The visual made her smile, as she was soaked between her legs. His fingers slid inside her easily as he kissed her mouth and face passionately. She groped awkwardly at his male member, which had hardened to the point of feeling like a steel rod in her hands. It was pulsating and hot. "Oh my God," she cried out as he suckled again at her breasts, tugging hard on them with his lips before biting at them hungrily. He mounted her, entering her without further hesitation. She gasped, quickly catching the rhythm of his fevered stroke.

That night in the backyard they'd worked quickly at the sex too. They went at each other hungrily like little animals scrambling quickly and quietly for food before something bigger caught them in the act. It was different this time, however, as Marcel moaned loudly. It was as if his body were in pain, aching for satisfaction that could only come from somewhere deep inside hers. She arched her hips upward, urging his search for release. Rising to his knees he held her slender hips, rotating them round and round, hitting all the spots before plunging in deep. She cried out, which seemed to only reheat his fire.

For longer than what Lacy was used to with any other lover, she and Marcel went at the act until finally after two or three deep thrusts Marcel released his passions.

Rolling off of her, he lay there, breathing heavily.

This was no accident.

Chapter 7

"I don't mean this in a bad way, Lace, but why would Phoebe give you the money from her insurance policy?" Marcel asked, taking a huge bite from his donut.

They had moved the coffee and sweets into her bed now. The dogs settled in at the foot, and Pete had simmered down to mild outbursts now and then.

"Marcel, you have to believe me when I say I have no idea. I mean, sure, as kids we used to say stuff like, 'oh I'll give you all my earthly possessions' and junk like that. I mean, at one time I even willed her all my stuff," Lacy admitted, slapping her forehead as if just remembering that little to-do on her life's list. She needed to get back with her attorney and change her will. *Oh, and Steven Prophet, the insurance adjuster.* He'd already called her and left a message. She had not returned the call simply because she thought his call had been a mistake. He hadn't been specific over the phone about what he really wanted. He had just identified himself as an insurance adjuster and told her to call him. Lacy thought it was a telemarketer and figured there was no rush to get back to it. Now she knew what he wanted, and with California being a community property state there was probably a real good reason he wanted to know why she considered Lacy next of kin. There truly was going to be a little red tape with her getting the money instead of Harold, or even Marcel for that matter.

No worries . . .

"I mean, the money would come in handy, I'm sure, but . . ." Marcel began.

Suddenly Lacy's mind wandered to Marcel's true motives for bringing up the policy. "Marcel, I don't need that money. You may need the money. But I don't. I'm doing well at my job and—" she began to fuss.

"Your job?"

Growing instantly offended, Lacy snapped, "My job."

"You're a cartoon, for crying out loud. That's not a job."

"And you're a pig," she said bluntly.

Marcel's eyes bugged out as he seemed now to have difficulty swallowing the sweet bread. "What?"

"Isn't that what they call you?"

"Yeah, back in the sixties. Damn! Serious attitude adjustment. What's that all about? Come on, I was joking."

"You started it," Lacy jibed before dusting the sugar from her hands.

"Anyway." He kissed her quickly on the lips, as if calling a truce before he continued. "Seriously, though, the more I thought about it the more it bugged me that she did that. I remember the little 'you'll get all I have on earth' thing you guys did, but that was kid stuff. This is grown-up, complicated shit that required intent. She actually made you a beneficiary of a very lucrative policy. That bugs me."

"Bugs me more how many people already knew she did it before me. I mean, how did you know about it? How did Denise know about it? I mean, everybody seemed to know about it but me!"

"Well, I knew about it because . . . well, because I'm a . . ." He paused. "Pig. It's my job to know about stuff. When my sister was killed, I immediately looked into everything. Including who would benefit from her be-ing dead."

Lacy shook her head. "Killed? You mean accident, and nobody is *benefiting* from that."

"Accident, yeah, that's what I meant," Marcel said, sounding less than convincing. He turned away.

Lacy turned his chin toward her face to get a closer look into his eyes. "You think she was killed?"

Marcel swallowed what appeared to be a thick lump in this throat, causing his Adam's apple to rise and fall. "Yes, and I think Harold did it. Somehow and for some reason—"

"But if he did it, he would have been stupid, too. I mean, he wasn't her beneficiary," Lacy interjected. "And if he killed her, he still wouldn't get any money. I mean, think about, surely he had to know too. I mean, Phoebe had been having accidents nearly yearly for a while and I'm sure their insurance company had them flagged. If Harold was the policy holder on this baby, it would have looked like"—Lacy took a gulp of air—"something other than what it was, an accident."

"Well I'm sure he assumed he wouldn't get caught for something other than an accident, and I have to figure, too, he also didn't know he wasn't getting paid."

Lacy leaned back to get a better look at Marcel's face and perhaps a clearer understanding of what he was implying. "He'd have to know, right? I mean, every-body did, right?"

Marcel hesitated as if he was thinking what he could not say. "Not really. Only the person who drew up the policy would know if she made changes at the last min-ute. That would be the family attorney, Adam Stillberg, and I've tried to get in to see him, but that mother-fucker isn't talking to me."

"Well with that attitude I wouldn't either." Lacy guffawed.

"Me? Attitude? Please, Ms. Man-Hatin' Queen of the Amazon." Marcel laughed. It was an obvious ploy to change the subject, but at this moment Lacy was up for it.

"Don't make me have your head removed," Lacy threatened playfully, reaching for Marcel's crotch. Marcel, looking serious now, stopped her hand as it grasped his manly member. "I'm just kidding!" Lacy said, feeling heat rise to her cheeks.

"No, it's not that. I'm . . . I'm," Marcel stammered. "Lacy, I'm sorta . . ."

Lacy knew what he was about to say. She felt it suddenly in her gut. She knew. "Where is she? I mean, how could you stay out all night without calling her or—"

"I did call. I lied and said I was with my parents. Lacy, I'm sorry. I'm sorry."

"What's her name? Is she your wife? I guess I would have heard about a wedding. Hell, my parents would have gone to your wedding and . . . and . . ." Lacy was starting to nervously ramble. "And Denise."

Marcel took her hand tightly. "She's a cop. We've been together for a long time and . . ."

Lacy's lips tightened over clinched teeth, forming a stiff smile. Marcel grew silent, running his fingers through his thick hair. As if sensing the tension the dogs stood and shook themselves. It was as if they were saying, "Well, buddy, time to go."

But Marcel refused to heed their body language. Instead, he reached for the back of Lacy's head, pulling her into a passionate kiss filled with tongue exploration. Lacy wanted to fight it but her heart could not and neither could her thighs. They parted as easily as the hot dog buns at a barbeque—receiving Marcel's link without even a slather of mustard to moisten them.

Panting and grunting they worked out their feelings—angry, embarrassing, lustful, hungry, needy feelings—and, in the end, they made . . . love.

Their passion was more than any passion Lacy had
ever known. They had no restraints. Turning her back
to him she held on to the headboard as he took her
from behind, tugging on her small breasts and biting
the back of her neck. On her back, her legs went over
his shoulders as he drilled her as if gold were to be his
reward in the end.

Lovemaking with Marcel was more fantastic than
she even fantasized about. There were no awkward
moments. Loud and vocal, she'd never felt so many
sensations before. She had never screamed and cried
out this way before. As the waves of pleasure rose and
peaked, ebbed and subsided, slamming against the
walls of her woman's cave like a wave of molten lava
making its way through a tunnel. She begged for more.
Perhaps this really was what an orgasm felt like.

The first one took her by surprise, but the second
and third came as old friends, familiar, yet quaking
her, rocking her, finally, moving her to tears. Marcel
seemed to have all the time in the world just for her to
experience each sensation she was having. With each
orgasm he seemed to applaud her with a smile of ap-
preciation.

"Let it cum, baby," he would say. "Just let it cum."

Finally, they climaxed together in one harmonic
symphony of passion that Lacy was sure could be heard
for miles.

Lying on top of her, Marcel said softly, "Your mother
thinks you're in love with me." Lacy did not respond, as
her mind spun to a place that was clear out of the world
they were in at the moment. "And well, I need to tell
you, I've been with Charla for a long time. I know I love

her. I think I do. I don't know. I mean, I did know, but now I don't," he finally admitted, running his fingers through her thick hair again before uncoupling himself from her tight cove.

Lacy, all but pushing him off of her, climbed quickly out of the bed and slid on her robe. The dogs too jumped up again as if realizing the concert was over, and rushed with her into the living room. Passing the large mirror over the mantel she saw her face, flush and filled with life, her eyes crazed and a shade of blue she had never seen before.

Smoothing back her wild hair, she realized she needed a strong drink. She could see his reflection coming from the room behind her. He had pulled on his pants and shirt, although the shirt was unbuttoned. His eyes were dark and nearly sinister. He was so very handsome she had to turn away from the mirror.

She wanted to hate him but what was the point? She knew then that she never would. "Please go," was all she could muster, and even those words came with a whisper.

"Lace—"

"Please . . ."

"You bastard!" Pete yelled out from under his blanketed cage. "I hate youuuuuu."

Chapter 8

Monday morning, the drive into the city was hectic and slow moving along the 680. Lacy reached the television station. Passing the receptionists, she was hit with an uncommonly huge smile. Heading down the steps to the studio she was then greeted by suspicious smiles that culminated upon her reaching the bottom step which flowed into the "pit." She'd have to cross the pit to get to the recording studio, crossing her desk in the path. She hardly needed a desk, at least one so out in the open, but the studio booth could get tight sometimes when all the voice-over actors would converge in there at once. So she asked for a desk and got one amid the news folks and on-air talent. *They are an interesting bunch,* she always thought. Nonetheless, the workplace was typical when it came to office politics and bureaucracy. Perhaps it was all the FCC governance that made everyone feel so . . . so . . . corporate.

Everyone generally pretended never to notice anything about anything or anyone, yet what was usual was everyone knowing everything about everything and everyone. It was the customary game to play.

Lacy had been sleeping with Gary. He worked in the sound department. He handled sound for both the local television shows, which she was a part of, and the local news shows. He was a tall, dark-haired white man with the palest of blue eyes and the most perpetual tan—real George Hamilton type of tan. Living in California, it should have been easy to get a more natural-looking one than he had but . . . whatever. It was clear that he opted for tanning booths, as he was evenly colored from head to toe.

Gary was one of few there who knew her father to be a dark-skinned black man. He didn't seem to care that she was racially mixed; nonetheless, Lacy often wondered if Gary was trying to be, in the most politically incorrect way, black. From the music he listened to, to the overly potent street slang he would attempt now and then, he seemed to be trying really hard to be what he was not.

Although they hadn't done much openly recreational together outside the office, she knew he liked to go clubbing at the black clubs in Oakland. He talked about it often when they would have dinner together in their favorite quaint, out-of-the-way restaurant. Gary talked a lot about his life during their time together, much more than Lacy talked about herself and her life. The most he knew was that her mother was Australian and her father was a former military man, and black. She hadn't even told him about Phoebe dying a couple of weeks before or the funeral just the other day. She sure as hell hadn't mentioned Marcel. It was hard enough to know why they were even dating than to get him mixed up in her personal affairs.

In the office, Lacy and Gary would pretend there was nothing going on, and so would everyone else. She and Gary would even leave in separate cars on the nights they would be together, meeting up as if happenstance at a restaurant that didn't require a reservation, and then leaving separately to meet up at the hotel, parting ways after just a few hours later. Lacy wasn't sure if their relationship had any real substance, but it had become comfortable for the time being. Either that or

Lacy had simply tired of trying to figure it out. They hadn't gone out in a while, and Lacy had started wondering if maybe Gary had given the "why are we doing this" some thought.

Sometimes Lacy would try to take away something pertinent from all the information he'd offered up about himself. She'd hope to take away something important to lovers so that later she could treasure it. She often tried to think of things such as the day they met, or his favorite color, but it would never come to her and, in the end, seemed so silly and pointless.

She and Marcel met the day her parents moved into the house: April 3, 1985. She was ten and he was twelve. His favorite color was maroon, his favorite food was fried chicken, and he loved the show *Dragnet*—the original one with Jack Webb. He sang in the shower and his favorite song was "Reach out of the Darkness," an oldie tune by the band Friend & Lover. Lacy smiled, realizing she knew about Marcel things that were truly important between lovers. Suddenly her mind went to his words: *I love her.* "Ugh," she groaned, unable to keep the sound inside.

"What's up, sweetie?" Doris asked, hearing her.

Lacy glanced at her before passing her by. "Nothing really, just a . . ." Lacy thought about her privacy and the unspoken rule of the office: don't tell anything; just let people figure it out on their own. "Nothing."

Now Doris flashed Lacy a knowing wink. Lacy saw it right before she walked on past toward her little desk, where she hoped to find the script for the day. "Already, Doris?" Lacy mumbled under her breath. The obtuse games didn't usually start until around Wednesday.

Lacy wondered about Doris's wink for a second longer until she reached her desk and saw the bouquet of pink roses waiting—her favorite rose. She glanced at

Gary, thinking perhaps she'd once said to him something about it being her favorite. Maybe he was coming out of hiding with their relationship. She slightly cocked her head in a questioning fashion in the direction of the bouquet, but he just pretended to be concentrating on a script he was holding. There was a card with the bouquet. The card read:

Lace, I really don't sleep with my gun. But I do need my handcuffs back.

Signed, Officer DuChamp.

Lacy giggled aloud. Of course the flowers weren't from Gary. He would have never made such a public commitment to her, and this was a commitment, right? Marcel loved her, right? No, he loved Charla. He told her that. Her emotional balloon deflated. She had to accept that she and Marcel would only be friends. They had something together when both of them needed friendship and comfort. He needed comfort that night the same way she had needed comfort the night he took her into his tent. They were even now. She'd have to accept that.

Suddenly, Lace felt hot, curious eyes on her. Glancing over her shoulder to check it out, she saw everyone around snap back to his or her business. "Uh," she began to announce, still holding the card, "the funeral. I went to a funeral and, well, he is the brother of my best friend who died, remember?" she continued as if she'd actually told anyone about the funeral and hadn't trusted that they all had their share of snooping into her personal notes left on her desk. "We grew up together. He was uhhh . . . uhh and we're just, you know, trying to keep things, you know . . . happy," she rambled on, offering more information than everyone acted as if they wanted to know. Waving their hands in disbelief and shaking their heads, different ones went back to their work—freely. It was as if they were disappointed in her self-exposure. It was as if she was ruining the game they so enjoyed playing. Suddenly, though, Lacy noticed Gary glaring at her angrily before he disappeared into the sound booth.

Jealous?

Later that day she asked him discreetly at the water cooler to join her for dinner. It wasn't as if she wanted to sleep with him. *Or maybe I do,* she thought. Deep inside she knew she needed to get over Marcel, and, well, Gary and a good roll in the sack might just do the trick. *Right?*

He childishly smirked. "Why don't you call Officer DuChamp?"

"You read my card?" *So much for Gary and the big waterbed hotel, and so much for him getting Marcel off my mind,* she thought.

Gary had become a comfortable addition to her life, which almost made her think twice before ending whatever it was they had. But reading her card? Oh yeah, he had crossed the line for sure with that one. He was acting like a boyfriend. He was acting entitled. Marcel was a little bit of information that was not on her list of things to share with him. True, Gary was great on the rack, but if that card and those flowers meant that something real was getting ready to start with Marcel, *it was great knowing you, Gary, but,* Lacy then reasoned, forgetting all about Charla for a moment.

"Everybody read your fucking card, Lacy," Gary whispered loudly, looking around after his silent rage settled a little. "You trying to make a fool of me or what?"

"What? No."

"Don't think . . . Don't ever think you can make a fool of me, ya little bitch."

"What? I know you didn't just call me that," Lacy snapped, slamming her hands on her hips. She was getting a little louder now.

"Oh, here it comes. What you gonna start doing now, jeckin' ya neck and goin' off? So this new guy, Marrrrrcelllll, is he black? Nah, can't be. DuChamp. Nah, sounds like a fuckin' dago," Gary said, sounding racist and stupid.

Lacy was instantly floored, and before she caught herself she slapped Gary hard across the face and stormed off. *So much for a graceful good-bye,* she thought.

Recording was tough that day. The producer called for five retakes, which was unusual for the session. Surely Gary had a lot to do with it. No time for breaks or to check her cell for calls from Marcel. But, then again, by the end of the day she saw there had been none. Between Gary's funky attitude and the producer's abusive rants over the retakes, and the beautiful, yet confusing, bouquet of flowers from Marcel, Lacy was emotionally exhausted and couldn't wait to get home.

Chapter 9

"So when were you gonna tell me about the flowers?"

"What flowers?" Marcel said, pouring sugar into his coffee.

Aretha flinched. She was always amazed at the amount of sugar Marcel used in his morning java. She would say, "Want a little coffee with your sugar?" It was just that much. "The flowers you sent to that woman who was not your girlfriend."

"I wasn't gonna tell you about those flowers I sent to the woman who is not my girlfriend, because it was none of your business about those flowers I sent."

"Uh-huh . . ."

"Besides, how do you know about that?"

Marcel and his partner were at it again. Aretha had been on the force for fifteen years. Most of her time had been served on the streets of Los Angeles, California, where she was born and raised. It was bad enough that her name was Aretha Franklin, which leant itself to enough harassment from Marcel, but over that time she'd gotten to be well known for her inherited intuitive skills and keen sense of observation. Those skills had gotten her further than any book. The ability to just "feel it" had also gotten her and him into a lot of jams with their superiors. Nonetheless, there wasn't a cop on the streets of Los Angeles who wasn't glad she had that gut instinct.

Aretha was nearing forty and, now divorced, she had decided to relocate to the Bay Area. The vibe was better, she had said, and the streets were a little calmer. Being from Los Angeles, she had been on a roller coaster ride every day. Nonetheless, in the last year and a half in this quiet community she had begun to feel a *yawn* coming on, and had been yearning for something more. She would chuckle and tease Marcel about how excited everyone at the station would get over a little thing like finding a body. But then Marcel told her about his sister's death and she perked up a bit.

She'd disappeared after a boating accident and was presumed lost at sea. Marcel wasn't buying it. He wasn't trying to even hear that she was dead, especially since none of her remains had shown up amid the particulate matter that had been gathered by the Coast Guard since the accident over two weeks ago. The funeral had taken place this past Saturday and Marcel had been acting a little shady since then—unusually so.

He hadn't said much about the funeral and she was planning to ask him about it later. It wasn't as if he was all broken up—hell, he didn't even believe she was dead. So she didn't feel as though she had to tiptoe around this whole case. In her mind, however, if the sister wasn't up to being dead, what was she up to? That, to Aretha, was the biggest question. Marcel, however, was not on the same page. He was looking everywhere but straight at his sister for clues as to what could be going on. Even now, he was still trying to get in touch with the insurance guy. Aretha had noticed that on his to-do list with the other investigative notes on his desk calendar. That's when she noticed the note about the flowers being sent that morning to a Lacy Durham. The name sounded familiar but it wasn't hitting any immediate bells.

Aretha pointed at the note. Aretha would have sworn in court that his face changed three shades of red instantly.

"Close friend of the family. Actually she's Phoebe's beneficiary on her life insurance," Marcel answered.

"That's a strange thing to know. How did you know before talking to the insurance guy?"

"Well, to be truthful, it's a strange thing for her to be. I mean, Lace and my sister are kind of an odd pair. Lacy grew up next door to us and would come around all the time, and Phoebe would just sort of, like, let her. It was like they ended up being friends more out of circumstance than planned effort."

"Girl next door . . ."

"Yeah. But you wouldn't call them best buds, but then, on the other hand, they have this like . . . connection," he explained.

Aretha watched his face light up as he spoke about the girl next door. He went on for a few more minutes before she knew all she needed to know. Marcel was in love with this woman Lacy Durham—*who he called Lace,* as if she didn't notice. He went on talking about this friendship between this Lace person and his sister, which didn't sound like a friendship to her. It sounded more like something convenient until the time was right for him and her to get together—like now. Like when the sister was finally out of the way—like now.

"And that connection was . . . ?" Aretha asked as if he really could not see the nose sitting on his face. It was obvious to her instantly—*You were the boy next door! The connection was you, dumb-dumb!*

"Have no idea. I just know there was something they both seemed to have in common and it kept them friends. I mean, Lace lived next door to us. Her folks and my folks are still neighbors and—"

Suddenly it came to her where she had heard the name. "Lacy Durham," Aretha now said aloud. "Afternoon, kid hour, you know . . . Saturday morning cartoons! She's the voice of Queen Hynata, the Amazon Queen and major man hater." It figured that Marcel would want the woman all men loved to hate. The thought made her shake her head again.

"What?" he asked, unable to hide his little boy smile that crept to the corners of his lips.

Just then the captain came out and handed them a notepad with addresses and names scribbled on it. "We got a body. Ugly scene. Looks like he's been dead longer than anybody should be. Get out there," he barked.

"Gotcha!" they both said, accepting the assignment without argument.

Along the way, Marcel continued to talk about growing up next door to Lacy Durham. His conversation was like doing the cha-cha: two steps forward and then three steps backpedaling. Let him tell it, she meant nothing. But let Aretha hear it—she was his soul mate if she had ever heard one described.

They reached the waterfront. "Got a name?" Aretha asked the officers on the scene.

"Boyd Jameson. I can't even say how he died, but this doesn't look natural to me," the officer answered, grimacing at the remains. Boyd's face was blistered and his mouth eaten away, as if by acid or some other chemical.

Aretha looked around for anything that may be a clue. She didn't see much to go on. "I don't even know what to say."

Marcel's nose wrinkled. He pointed at empty fast food containers nearby. "I say if it was his lunch that did this, he had some serious acid indigestion!"

Aretha tried not to laugh.

Chapter 10

Steven Prophet, the insurance investigator, had called again. This time he had specifically stated that he wanted to discuss Phoebe Kitchener's insurance policy. This was the second call since the funeral. He was worse than a telemarketer, in Lacy's opinion. But at least she knew what he wanted.

The beneficiary issue. "Gosh I don't want to talk about that," Lacy said aloud, listening to the voice mail. She hadn't answered the call when it came. Needless to say, the number didn't look familiar so she hadn't answered it. She wasn't even thinking that it could have been Marcel calling. It wasn't as if she had his phone number. It wasn't as if she knew how to get a hold of him, beyond asking his parents. "And I'm not going to ask them. I mean, what would I say? Me and Marcel slept together and now I need to call him but I don't know how to find him. That would sound great."

"I hate youuuuuu," Pete bellowed.

"You know, you really should teach that nasty birdie some manners," Lacy heard someone say to her through the open sliding door. She jumped. Dave, her neighbor, burst into laughter. "My, my, aren't we rather skittish," he added.

Lacy smiled weakly. She wanted to blurt out what had her nerves on end but she couldn't. It involved Marcel. She wasn't ready to even say his name again. Sure, she'd known Dave since moving into the house.

He'd become what most would probably consider a friend, but friendship was relative to Lacy. She realized that now. What did she know about friends? She didn't know Phoebe was a movie star. She didn't know Marcel was living with some woman. What did she know about anything or anybody?

Sure, she and Dave hung out. Dave walked her dogs and looked after her bird when she had to travel to her folks', even though her mother actually liked Pete. Sarah, Lacy's mother, claimed Pete spoke to her on a regular basis, and not just curse words, either. She claimed that Pete told her things about Lacy's personal life. She swore to it that Pete filled her in, as it were. Lacy just took it as a major hint that she didn't call home enough. She refused to feed her mother's guilt trip by giving in and making promises she had no intention of keeping—like dinner on Sundays or even minor holidays, for that matter. Of course, a major one was coming up soon and Lacy was going to have to plan for it. Okay, so it was only Halloween, but that was major in her mother's book.

"Well, I all but thought you had faded to black," Lacy said to the former thespian. Dave had been a stage actor for many years before his agent pushed a new medium. But television wasn't kind to him and forced his retirement ten years ago at the ripe old age of fifty. Since then he'd pondered a return to the stage, but after meeting Lacy he turned his energies to the visual arts and started painting, writing, and teaching both mediums at the local adult school in town. He saw how she had flourished behind the camera and through the uses of her creative writing. He figured he could do the same.

"Me? No. I've been busy, I guess you could say," Dave answered while stepping into her dining area through the door. The dogs greeted him with their usual disinterest. Dave was another person the dogs were okay with. Lacy thought about their ease with Marcel. Maybe they weren't as ferocious as she had made them out to be. But, then again, Dave was with them often—sort of—lately.

"Busy?" Lacy said, noticing his slight blush.

"Yes. Busy. I've been busy falling in love."

"Really?" Lacy said, reserving her own love short story for a time when and if it may have been more story than short.

"Well, you wouldn't even believe me if I told you about it, so I will spare you the details, but suffice it to say that she fell into my life like an angel from heaven—actually, she fell on the cliffs. Don't ask, but then she disappeared the same way." Dave's tone changed only slightly. Lacy could tell he was not happy about the disappearance of the woman, the angel, the fantasy, or whatever she was. He'd apparently had a party. She had thought he'd stopped entertaining drunks and actors who did nothing but bellyache about their dying careers. She'd thought those days were long behind him—that's what he'd told her. But finding a woman unconscious on the cliffs sounded like the leftovers of a party to her.

"So you've met someone?"

"Yes and no. I never even got her name. We spent a week together and I never even knew her name."

"Wow!"

"Yeah, you can say that again. She was . . . She was . . . very . . . Wow," Dave exploded after grappling with words to describe the woman. "I have never been with a woman so fantastic. I mean, the sex was—"

"Whoa! You slept with a complete stranger?"

"Lacy, she was in my home for a week. She was in my bed for a week. Come on now. I'm old but not dead or particularly bad looking," Dave added.

Lacy felt the heat rise to her face. She had never really considered Dave in that way before. He and she just never clicked that way. But, then again, Lacy wondered if she really clicked with anybody. Her mind went back to the disaster she called her day.

"Me and Gary broke up," she said. Dave was the only one she'd told about Gary.

Dave smirked as if to say "about time," and moved past her to her liquor cabinet. "Let's drink to it," he said.

"What? Gary or your angel?"

"Hell, both," he said. Suddenly, he shook his head as if remembering something. "Damn, I didn't even ask you about the funeral. I mean, was it hard to get through? I'm sorry I wasn't here for you."

Lacy's face grew hot again. "It was fine," she said, avoiding the mention of Marcel. Marcel was where the secret sharing stopped between the two of them. Dave knew nothing about Marcel. Actually, she hadn't even said his name out loud to Dave before.

Dave cocked his head to the side as if trying to read her blush. "Hmm, okay. Well, sit, sit, and let me tell you about my angel."

Lacy retrieved the glass from him and sat on the sofa. "Dave, you can't even tell me her name."

"It isn't her name that I fell in love with," he remarked, sounding naughty and sexually heated.

Chapter 11

Steven Prophet looked over the case that lay on his desk. It had been a couple of weeks since he'd reviewed it. The file bothered him. From the moment it landed in his hands it felt bothersome. It was an insurance claim for double indemnity, paying out over a million dollars. He'd only seen one other payout this large in his career as an insurance adjustor. Even then, his company fought it tooth and nail until finally they had to give up and pay it.

Many people buy policies such as this, but rarely do they pay off. Usually it's just a ploy by insurance companies; giving people the thought that they are worth a million dollars sells policies. But, generally, double indemnity death collection is rare. But when it does come up, it's a bear to wrestle with and it's sad on both ends and equally frustrating.

First off, you pay for the policy and, therefore, you expect it to pay when something happens, but, then again, something has to happen to you before it will pay, he thought, reviewing the notes. In this instance, the worst of all kinds of tragic accidents had taken the life of a beautiful woman named Phoebe Kitchener. Nothing seemed out of sorts on the claim, short of the fact that it was due to pay out so much money. Therefore, Steven's boss put him on the case. He was good at making sure every i was dotted and every t was crossed before the company handed over the money. He was good at not paying off claims. He was even better at finding fraudulent claims and nipping them in the bud. *But that's why they pay me the big bucks,* Steven said with a sigh as he thought about the trek out to the site of the accident.

Mr. Kitchener had been calling nonstop since he was notified that he was not the beneficiary of the policy. *You'd think the guy would be mourning somewhere instead of bugging me for money. It's not like she's even been dead a month!* Steven thought before filling his mouth with the remainder of the Gummy Bears his three-year-old daughter had left on his desk when she was there the day before. He smiled as he thought about her face.

Steven's wife, Breezy, had died the year before of an inoperable brain tumor. Doctors had discovered it during her pregnancy with their daughter, Brianna.

Breezy had been so brave near the end. The thought of losing his wife was hard to accept. The thought of Harold Kitchener wishing his wife dead so as to benefit from her death made Steven sick. But the more he thought about Harold's eagerness to collect the money, the more he felt that Harold was looking to profit off his wife's death. *But why? Why is he so eager to take the money from the person whom his wife decided to be beneficiary? It's not like he had children to support. I could understand that if the wife had left him with a bunch of kids and no money. But that's not the case,* Steven pondered. And who was this Lacy Durham? Maybe she needed the money. So what that she wasn't blood related—which was kind of strange in a way that Phoebe Kitchener left her the money, when all Harold would have had to do was make a claim for it.

So there must be a reason Phoebe wanted this Lacy woman to have it, Steven went on thinking.

Looking over the report again, Steven decided then he wasn't going to just allow this guy to collect the money easily. He was going to have to work for it; besides, the fact was that Phoebe Kitchener left it to a woman named Lacy Durham. She'd not called about it or asked when she would get paid. She had not even called him back after he'd left a message last week. She didn't seem worried about it.

There must have been a reason Phoebe trusted her to do the right thing with all that money. She must have felt that Lacy Durham deserved it more than her own husband.

Steven knew he'd need to get his bias regarding Harold Kitchener under control. He was going to have to make a fair assessment of the situation.

"Steven, you have that appointment," his secretary said, entering his office.

"Oh yeah, the scene of the crime," Steven said, sounding mysterious.

She frowned slightly as if not really understanding him. "Crime? You mean accident. Steven, you've been watching too much TV again. You're an insurance investigator, not Columbo," she said, adding a chuckle on the end of her words.

Chapter 12

Again he dreamed of her, only it couldn't be her. She had been dead for just about a month now. But the dreams were so real that they were frightening him. Harold's dream last night was the weirdest yet. Had he not known better, he'd have said he was being taken captive by aliens during the night and taken to the world of Phoebe. Some nights she would fuck him, other nights she would all but torture him, scratching at him, pulling his hair, threatening his life. He would only dream of her when he wouldn't spend the night with Victoria.

Like tonight . . .

Tonight, he'd come in from work and had his regular glass of wine while lying in bed. He had contemplated taking a skinny Victoria dip but decided against calling her. She was starting to bore him. Adam had been hesitant in going along with Harold's thoughts regarding sexual exploration with Victoria. *And maybe Adam is right. Victoria is a bit square—she is nothing like Phoebe when it comes to sex,* Harold thought. Phoebe was a freak—all her friends were. Well, at least the ones he'd had. Okay, so he'd only had a couple . . .

Anyway, back to the dream . . .

Last night she brought a knife and held it over his head while she rode his dick mercilessly. She'd tied his hands to the headboard and . . . and, yeah, he was remembering it now. She'd tied his hands, sucked him until he was hard, and then rode him until she came, all while holding a knife over his head.

He'd told Victoria that it wouldn't look right for them to take up cohabiting in the house he shared with Phoebe so soon after Phoebe's death, and especially while in the process of fighting the insurance policy to pay off. "I need to be grieving. You know that," he explained over the phone. Victoria was angry with him but it was what it was. Harold had spoken to Adam about Victoria. Adam had scared him with the talk about going to court. Collecting the insurance money shouldn't have been this hard to do.

Adam had made out the policy. Didn't he know Phoebe was naming Lacy the beneficiary? But, then again, had he argued with her she may have gotten wise to what was really going on. Adam was a sly one when it came to working things out for the benefit of all those involved. He must have known they would win hands down in court against Lacy Durham.

"She doesn't have a leg to stand on. Phoebe didn't even like her really. She was just someone to whine to. She was a . . . What did Phoebe call her?" Harold thought aloud now. "A clumsy, skinny little loser who actually thinks my brother would want her." Harold laughed. "Boy, it sure ate Phoebe alive when that chick got that slot on TV. It was so easy after that to talk her into making those dirty movies. Phoebe was always such a jealous bitch," he said aloud to himself with a wicked snicker following.

Looking at his watch, he saw it was a little after three A.M. Sliding on his robe he headed to the bathroom. Suddenly, he felt a sharp pain in his thigh. "Ouch!" he yelped, grabbing at it. Pulling back his hand he noticed the blood. "What the . . ." he gasped, looking down at the hurt area. There was a small gash, the size of what would be made with a small blade, like one the size of a paring knife. "Fuck! What is this?" he asked, rushing into the bathroom, opening his medicine cabinet. "How in the hell did I do this?" he asked himself as the pain now grew with the realization of the source. Applying hydrogen peroxide, he examined the cut to deduce his need for stitches. He didn't need any but it hurt like hell for sure. "Shit!" he gasped, searching for Band-Aids now.

Just then the phone rang. Limping quickly to his bedside he saw the call was from Victoria. "Hey, Vick, wow, just in time. I have something freaky to tell you; can you come over? I need you."

"No, I'm just sick, Harold. I'm so disgusted. I saw one of those movies."

"What? Where? I mean, what movie?"

"Adam's office. I was in there tidying up some things and I found it. I have never been so disgusted in all my life! How could you produce something so vile?"

Harold realized then that she must have found one that he wasn't in. She obviously didn't recognize Adam and the women, either. "Oh now, Victoria, please, let me explain. I told you a long time ago, me and Phoebe—"

"Oh my God, why did you say her name to me? Adam told me that was her in the movie! Adam told me that you let her be in movies like that . . . That you . . ." Victoria was obviously crying now. "How could you watch your wife do that with another man?"

"Oh, Vick, you have to understand. It was a business. I'm not in that business anymore. That was a long time ago," he lied.

"You told them to do . . . You told them to do such vile things. I heard your voice, and to think I let you . . . that

I let you . . . humiliate me like you did. When you filmed us making love you said you'd never done anything like that before. You said I was special." Victoria was nearly hysterical now. "Oh my God, not only did you lie, you . . . Oh forget it. You're just so vile. So perverted. I can't be with you anymore."

"I don't want to break up. I love you. I do."

"No. You don't. You want to use me the way you apparently used Phoebe, and I'm not going to do it."

"I'm coming over there. I need to know what the hell is going on."

"Don't bother. I'm done with you and all this madness." Victoria was whimpering. "I thought what we had was special. But I found pictures, Harold. I found pictures of you and some redheaded woman. You had sex with some redheaded woman—who is she? In the picture your head was between her thighs! Who is she?"

"Victoria, no, those pictures had to be fakes. I need to see them and—"

"I burned them and I never want to see you again," Victoria yelled into the phone. "And to think I let you do . . ." Victoria paused. "Do that thing to me." She hung up.

Harold sat stunned for a moment, thinking about his past dreams—the erotic dreams. Phoebe with red hair. Why she had red hair in the dream he didn't know. He had to figure he had blended visions of Lacy with Phoebe. He wasn't stupid. He knew a little about psychology and stuff, and that's what he figured. He thought about the pictures. He knew who the woman in the red wig was in the pictures, and it wasn't Phoebe but surely she couldn't be the woman he was dreaming about. The dreams were far too real. The woman in the dream was Phoebe . . . Hell, the woman in his condo was Phoebe—*forget dreams. This shit is real,* he thought, rubbing the wound on his leg. He picked up the phone to call Adam.

Chapter 13

"I gotta go, Harold, it's the middle of the night," Adam said, trying to put sleepiness in his voice while she gestured for him to hang up.

"I think Phoebe is alive. I think she's really alive."

"You're crazy, Harold. She's dead. She's really dead. I think you're having some last-minute guilt trip or something. Go to sleep."

"Victoria broke up with me tonight. She said—"

The woman moved over, rubbing Adam's bare, hairy chest before sensually licking his cheek, causing him to squirm in his readiness. "My God, Harold, I really gotta let you go."

"But, Adam, I—"

Adam hung up the phone. "Harold is going nuts," he said to the woman, moving to where he could grab hold of one of her breasts.

"It doesn't matter. You just need to make sure Lacy gets that money. I don't give a flying fuck about Harold," she purred before moving away from Adam and sitting up in the bed. She had on a red satin teddy with easy accessibility and Adam was ready for access.

"Why? Why would you care if Lacy got the money? Lacy getting it means Harold doesn't get it, and I'm of the mind that you wanted Harold to get it. I hate to sound naïve but I'm slightly confused now," Adam said, sounding as if he was losing patience with the conversation. He was ready for action. "So are you changing the plans or what?"

"Look, it's not for you to ask me questions. Just do what I'm asking you to do," she said. "But, yes, we've had some changes come up and we need the money now."

Adam wanted to talk about Steven Prophet, the insurance investigator, but there was no way he was going to upset this woman at a time like this. He had this situation covered. Sure, things could start to get dicey with an investigator on the case, but he figured this could happen. He'd already calculated that they may not just hand over a cool million dollars to the spouse of a porn actress, who'd disappeared under suspicious circumstances. He had a feeling that somebody might do some background checking, or even a private investigator might be hired to get a closer look at his involvement with the not-so-happy home of litigious swingers—Harold Kitchener and his accident-prone wife.

Adam Stillberg knew he was breaking the law every time he filed a lawsuit on Phoebe's behalf. Car accidents, food poisonings at restaurants—even a fall that lost her a baby in miscarriage. It was crazy what Harold was willing to do to that woman for money. They weren't content with just using her body in film. They had gotten just plain ol' ingenious. But Phoebe seemed to enjoy the acting. She had always wanted to be an actor. Unfortunately, her last performance didn't turn out quite the way she had planned. Yes, Adam was in over his head now, and things were coming to an end. He could feel it. Nonetheless, there had been very exciting detours during this entire journey and this was about to be one of them.

At that Adam gave into his true desires and pulled the woman into an embrace. "I love it when you get demanding."

"Really? Does it make you want to fuck me?"

"Oh yeah, in a real nasty way."

"Would you do anything to fuck me?"

"You know it," Adam growled, going for her neck to give a little love bite. She moved back.

"Then I want you to get Harold out of the way."

"What? What does that mean, out of the way?"

"And I also want you to stop seeing your girlfriend," she said, adding a sneer on the word "girlfriend."

"What? No, now that wasn't part of the deal. You said I could have you both no problem, and, well . . . frankly, she's not been holding up her end of this deal very well either. I think you should be talking to her about that."

"What? You're not man enough to handle both your women, Adam," she said, playfully biting his cheek as he sat up in the bed and pulled down the straps of the teddy, releasing her perfect breasts. His eyes got full of them before his hands took over the task. She leaned back, allowing him to fondle them freely. Reaching between his legs, she tugged on his short but thick, hairy manhood.

Adam purred, his eyes drooping sexily. "You gonna let me put it in your ass, baby? My *girlfriend* always let me do her like that—"

"Hell no," she said, moving back from him.

He grabbed her hand and put it back on his growing erection. Kissing her on the mouth, he then whispered in her ear, "You want the cameras on, baby. You wanna fuck daddy with the cameras on."

"Oh yeah, I love it when the camera is on. But first promise me you'll do what I want. I want you to make some changes for me."

"Anything, baby. Oooh, you're such a naughty girl, I'ma have to give you a spanking," he said, rushing to the dresser where the camera sat ready to film. He clicked the on button and turned back to the woman, who had pulled the teddy off and now waiting on all fours, wagging her hiney as if she were a dog greeting his master. "Oh yeah, come spank me just the way mama likes it," she growled.

Adam rushed back over to the bed just in time to give her a firm smack on her hindquarters, which left a red handprint. "Ouch, you bastard," she fussed. "Do it again."

He smacked her again.

Just then the door opened and Sonja walked in. "What the fuck!" she yelped.

"Ooopsy," the woman on the bed cooed. She seemed to be feeling too good to even get mad at the interruption.

Adam, on the other hand, jumped to his feet. "Sonja!"

"Don't give someone the key if you don't expect them to drop in . . . stupid," she fussed. The woman laughed wickedly, flopping back onto the bed on her back, allowing her legs to fall far apart. "You bitch," Sonja said to her before walking to the bed and pulling at her nipple. The woman squealed as if in pain or pleasure, Adam wasn't sure, but his erection grew painfully stiff now.

"Now, ladies, don't fight," Adam said, sounding less than convinced that a catfight might not be entertaining. To his surprise, however, instead of a fight, Sonja grabbed the woman by the back of the head and pulled her head up into an open-mouth kiss—tongue and all. Adam's mouth dropped open. He'd never seen two women make love in real life. He'd never been a part of a threesome, either.

"You were supposed to wait for me, you bitch," Sonja growled at her. "But no, you came early. You're greedy and you deserve to be punished," Sonja added.

The woman grinned and nodded in agreement. "But only if you do it," she told Sonja, who now turned to Adam, who was all but panting in his lust. Slowly Sonja unbuttoned the white shirt, exposing a leather bra with studs. A silver chain linked through one of the studs and traveled down her thin waist. As she slid from her skirt, Adam could see the chain connecting to a leather garter. She wore no panties, only the garter belt, which held up fishnet stockings. Had he been set up? Was this planned?

After she undressed she went back to the woman on the bed, fondling her breasts, and kissing her stomach. Adam moved up behind Sonja, who was now fully involved in kissing and fondling the other woman. She was headed toward the woman's middle when he rubbed her narrow hips, hoping for an invite. "Not my ass," Sonja said quickly between hungry kisses—stopping him dead in his plan.

The woman positioned herself now to receive Sonja's oral attentions between her legs. Sonja, while indulging her, bent over for Adam to enter her from behind, doggie style. Sonja was holding the woman at the waist, allowing the woman's breasts to rest on the top of her head. While in that position she took over at the other woman's crotch. Sonja was very flexible.

It was a scene out of only one of the best of porn films, as far as Adam was concerned, and he only hoped he had enough battery life.

"All we need now is Harold to walk in," the other woman said as she tugged at her own breasts.

"He better not," Adam said, looking around nervously, increasing his stroke speed to match his growing nervousness.

Both women burst into laughter.

Sonja looked back at him over her shoulder. "Then you better work a little faster, Adam."

"Okay, okay," he said, misunderstanding her meaning and now rushing his sexual stroke. Sonja was like an oven inside, tight and on fire.

"I don't mean fucking, I mean getting Harold out of the way," she said.

"Harold? Get Harold out of the way?" Adam tried to focus on her words but he couldn't. He couldn't give a good gottdamn about Harold right now. He was in heaven. He was pounding against Sonja's backside at jackhammer speed. Suddenly he gave her rump a swat. At that the other woman reached over Sonja's back and slapped him.

"Don't do that to her. Don't you ever hit her."

"But she likes that. Don't you, Sonja?"

Sonja rose up enough for the other woman to suckle at her breast. "No, I like this," Sonja purred, moving her breasts so that the woman would suckle between the both.

"I like your girlfriend, Adam," the woman said, grinning at him with Sonja's nipple in her mouth.

Adam about lost his mind. "Can I fuck you now?" he asked. She looked down at Sonja, who moved away from Adam's coupling. The woman opened her legs wide on the bed as if inviting Adam in. Adam nodded before wildly plunging between her legs.

Moving closer, Adam saw the woman's fingers disappear into Sonja's cove as Sonja began to grunt and pant to the rhythm of his hard thrusts. Adam was losing control in his excitement. He cried out in the passion that was driving him insane. Loud and sweaty, he finally came before pulling out of the woman.

Sonja then moved into his spot, feasting at what was left of the woman's desire. Adam was amazed and stood watching her complete the act of love with the woman whose head went back in orgasm with Sonja lapping between her legs. Sonja then climbed on top of the woman to allow the woman to return the favor on her. The woman held her thighs tight while sucking hard on Sonja's lower lips and dipping her tongue in and out. Sonja came with a squeal of pleasure. Adam watched then as the two women lay on top of one another, kissing and caressing and pressing their muffs together until they both began to writhe with a second orgasm of their mutual creation.

Chapter 14

Lacy had been having a hard time. She couldn't get Marcel off her mind. She wanted to be like other modern women who could just have sex and move on, but she couldn't this time. Not with Marcel. What she had shared with Marcel went beyond sexual. It was magical.

Gary was a man she could have sex with and then just go on as if she had just brushed her teeth, but with Marcel, she'd made love. She'd had the big O over and over for the first time in her life. She'd cried out in passion and . . .

"Ooooh God," Lacy gasped, all but bursting into tears. She fought them back with all her might. Lacy had run across one of the roses she'd saved from the bouquet today while at work. She'd smashed it between the pages of the novel she'd written. She kept a copy at work in case she needed to remember that she indeed had other talents then just being a voice-over for a cartoon. "Okay, so the cartoon is paying for the house, but the book paid the down payment," she used to say to anyone who challenged her writing talents.

Reaching for her cell phone, she needed to talk to Marcel. "I don't even have his number," she whimpered. "I know," she sniveled. "I'll call Denise. Denise knows everything about everything. She'll have his number. I know she'll have his number." Lacy's sobs turned to slobbers as she simpered while madly searching through her contacts. As soon as she found Denise's number she pushed the button, but the connection was interrupted by an incoming call. "Hello? Who is this?" she asked, trying to keep the cry out of her voice.

"Hello, Ms. Durham. This is the Half Moon Bay Realtors. You know, the company that sold you your home."

"Oh . . . Yes, yes. How can I help you?"

"Well, it's time to have your ducts inspected."

"My ducts. I'm sorry, all my ducts are in a row," Lacy said, surprising herself at her own humor. Okay, so maybe she was just premenstrual before. She was feeling okay now. But, then again, she'd popped a piece of chocolate from her candy jar in her mouth.

The woman laughed on the other end. "Oh, what a wit. I was hoping we could come by and inspect tomorrow."

"I work tomorrow. I won't be home."

"Oh, but we don't need you to be home."

"I have dogs. They bite, so . . . yeah, I need to be home."

"Do you have someone who can be there and, perhaps, let us in or take the dogs? This is so very important to your home's equity and warranty arrangement."

"I have a warranty on my home?" She felt stupid about these types of things, but her father had helped her buy the house. He'd taken care of all the legalities of buying the house, she'd just provided the money and she *so* didn't really care about things such as warranties. *That's what fathers are for, right?*

"Most definitely."

Lacy sighed. She didn't want to go to work tomorrow. She wanted to call in sick and stay home and cry over Marcel. She wanted to drink and cuss at Pete, but now even that plan was being interrupted. "Fine.

Yes, come by tomorrow. I'll have my neighbor take the dogs. Or be here with them . . . one or the other. I'm not really crazy about you being here in my home while I'm not here. So, yeah . . . that will work."

"Sorry you don't trust us."

"It's not that. It's—"

"It's not a problem. We get that often. We do understand. We'll call you when we arrive and when we leave, okay?" the woman asked.

"Yeah, sure, thanks," Lacy acquiesced. She figured she'd just ask Dave to watch the house while they were there.

Hanging up, Lacy had pushed the red end button and again started to call Denise, only to this time be interrupted by Harold. She didn't know the number but, again, her button pushing had connected her before she wanted to be connected. But, then again, maybe it was Marcel. Maybe he had read her mind, her heart. "Hello. Marcel?"

"Marcel? Marcel DuChamp? No, this is Harold."

"Harold?"

"Harold Kitchener."

"Oh my God, what do you want?" Lacy sighed, throwing two more pieces of chocolate in her mouth.

"I need to talk to you."

"About what?"

"Everything. Phoebe, the insurance policy, everything. Some strange shit is going on and we need to talk about it."

"I don't want to talk to you about anything. You can talk to my attorney," Lacy said, lying about having an attorney. She hadn't sought counsel. She hadn't even spoken to Steven Prophet. She hadn't even told her father about this situation. She had just wanted this whole money thing to die. She hoped it had died. At first it seemed like it was going to be such a biggo issue, but then when nothing happened after the first couple of weeks following the funeral, she just figured that everything had worked itself out. Harold's call told her it hadn't.

"Lacy, we don't need to bring attorneys in on this. You just need to call Adam Stillberg and tell him you don't want the money. He'll contact the insurance company, they'll have you sign something, and this will be over. If you don't, we'll just go to court and the judge will make you sign it. So just do it. But that's not what I called to talk about."

"The hell it isn't. I know all about you, Harold. I know you're a snake and that money is exactly what you called about, so good-bye," she said, hanging up. Staring at Denise's number, she wondered now if calling her would be such a good idea. She was upset and Denise would just go on a tangent about ways to get back at Harold. She wasn't up for the game. Instead, she tossed the phone onto the sofa and headed to the kitchen to look for food. She was starving.

Entering the kitchen, she opened the fridge. "I can't believe I don't have any Chinese food in here," she yelped. It would take a half hour to get down the hill and to the closest Chinese food restaurant. Looking out the window, she saw that the rain began to threaten the mild skies. "Hell, it's worth it for some shrimp chow mein." She ran to the living room, slipped back into her jacket, and with her two dogs riding along for protection, she flew down the hill for food. This wasn't the first time this week she'd done this, nor would it be the last.

Chapter 15

The woman sat watching Lacy barrel down the hill. She looked neither left nor right. "Now, she's got dogs, but I got this," the more aggressive woman said, holding up a dog repellent she'd gotten from the pet store.

"Will it hurt the dogs?"

The more aggressive woman burst into laughter. "The things that you worry about. We're getting ready to totally commit murder and you're fuckin' worried about some damn dogs."

"Murder? You said it would make her sick. You didn't say it would kill her."

"Sick, dead . . . whatever. Adam says we can't get the money until she's the latter," the woman pointed out. "Helloooo!"

"I . . . I don't like this."

"Since when? You've always wanted her dead. Ever since she fucked Marcel, and now, whether you wanna face it or not, sweetie, they're fuckin' again . . . and right after the funeral, too—so much for missing Phoebe!" The aggressive woman started up the car and continued up the hill to Lacy's house. "Now, we'll go in, putting this mercury in the central air ducts, and that's that. She blows air or heat, she'll be dead within a few weeks . . ." She looked over at her now passive partner. "Oh sorry, she'll get real sick and just hand over the money," she said before bursting into laughter.

"I can't believe you've actually timed this."

"Somebody had to. Good things don't just happen by accident."

Chapter 16

Steven headed down the steps to the boathouse. He needed to speak with Barry Nugent, the owner of the *Jewel*—the boat involved in the incident. Barry had insured the boat, but hadn't been paid as of yet from his insurance company. It seemed that the police and their forensics team were having a time with a few issues surrounding some residue found on a few of the boats' remains floating on the water. That, along with the fact that he was not on the boat when it went up, was enough to delay his payment and hasten an investigation.

"Why was Mrs. Kitchener on the boat alone?" Steven asked, again referring to his notes. He liked reading directly from the notes. It always made him seem official and he never had to quibble with people.

"It's a charter," Barry answered. "She and the mister paid for the time. He was licensed, so who was I to worry that they were gonna blow the dang thing up?"

"But the police are looking at possible arson?"

"No." Barry shook his head vehemently. "They are ruling that out. Read the report, guy! Ain't nothing shady going on here. It's a clear case of an accidental death. I mean, I lost a boat in all this. You think I would have torched my own boat with people on it? No, it's my livelihood."

"Yes, I understand that, and that would have been murder," Steven added, trying to keep this conversation in perspective. "Remember that. Someone did die on your boat, so not only would it be arson, it would be murder. But you're right, I'm sure it's just a formality."

"Yeah," Barry sighed nervously.

"So did you know Mrs. Kitchener prior to this day?" Steven asked regarding the day the boat went up.

"No."

"So did you just rent out your boat without any previous interviews or whatever?"

"Interviews? I'm not hiring them. I'm taking their money and lending them my boat, which, by the way, was a fucked-up situation this time, as they only paid half upfront and then my boat was blown to holy hell, and now my insurance isn't paying. When do I get compensated? When do I get some money outta this?"

"Mr. uh . . ." Steven glanced at his notes again. "Barry, uh . . . a woman died."

"I know that! But I need to be compensated!" Barry screeched. He was filling with emotion and Steven couldn't really read it. All he knew was that this man's attitude was similar to Mr. Kitchener: *just gimme the money; to hell with Phoebe Kitchener*. This whole thing was making Steven sick.

"I don't know, Mr. Nugent, but they just buried Mrs. Kitchener a couple of weeks ago, so I'm sure they will get to your situation soon."

"What about the husband? He didn't die?"

Steven's stomach tightened with the question. Why was he asking, and with such a blasé attitude, too? It made Steven force his mind off the tone of the man's voice and immediately on to something more pleasant. He thought about the sound of his wife, Breezy, and her laughter. He missed her with all his might. He felt so empty. He felt so much pain for his daughter's loss, more so than even his own. These men couldn't care less about that woman Phoebe and the fact that she had died. Who cared that she wasn't somebody's mother? She was a woman somebody loved . . . right? She was somebody's daughter. She was somebody's friend. She was somebody's sister.

Steven made a mental note to have lunch with Marcel DuChamp, Phoebe's brother. He just wanted to know the woman Phoebe Kitchener. He wanted to understand her a little better. It seemed like a simple thing—she died and made a friend her beneficiary, but it just didn't feel that simple.

Besides, Phoebe Kitchener's brother was a cop. Surely if there was truly something to this case he would be the first to go looking for it, right?

First Harold Kitchener and his stinking, greedy attitude, and now Barry Nugent, and Lacy Durham wouldn't even talk to him. Somebody needed to straighten some things out in his mind. He couldn't just stay out of this personally. He felt that his decision was going to change lives.

"Well, Mr. Nugent, unless they find anything fraudulent, your claim should be okay," Steven said, hoping for a response from Barry. The widening of his eyes told him all he needed to know. This case was not what it seemed and it probably was going to be even less of what Steven wanted it to be.

Feeling the vibration on his cell phone he checked the call. It was a familiar number. It was Adam Stillberg, the Kitcheners' attorney. "What does he want?" Steven said, climbing into his car.

Chapter 17

Marcel glanced over at his partner as soon as the captain disappeared into his office. He knew what she was going to say. She'd been saying it for weeks now. "I can't just let it go," he said before she even opened her mouth.

Shaking her head, Aretha held up her hand and fought back a smile.

"But you are not going to get anyone to give you the green light to investigate this. You're gonna have to let it do its thing officially," she told Marcel when he first started trying to get the case looked at a little closer. *"You're also gonna have to quit punching out suspects before they even become suspects, or you're gonna end up a suspect if something happens to that guy."*

He hadn't listened—of course not then and not now. He was gonna flatten Harold like a pancake anytime he was near that idiot and he opened his mouth to say anything foul about Phoebe, anytime he was near Lacy and harassing her like he did that day he followed him from Lacy's building after watching him trying to jam her up in the lobby.

Besides, they were threatening to close the case. It was going to be written off as an accidental death and filed away. He couldn't just sit back and let that happen. "I'm gonna talk to him again. I just need a couple of months."

"Marcel . . ." Aretha let his name hang. He was sure his glare stopped her from saying more. Her eyes followed him as he rose from his seat on the opposite side of the desk from her. He followed the captain's trail into his office.

Almost as if he were expected, the captain didn't even look up, but instructed him to close the door behind him.

"We have to close this, DuChamp. We have nothing pointing to murder. All we've got is some sloppy insurance work, but that's about it. The fire guys and water guys are wrapping it up pretty fast too. They can't prove arson, so we're nowhere. They can't prove anything foul happened on that boat."

"I can believe they can't prove it but that doesn't mean it didn't happen. I think they shouldn't be looking for arson or anything so simple. I think they should be looking for my sister." Marcel had learned to keep his cool when talking to the captain about this. It was a conversation they'd been having for about six weeks now, and he was learning how to handle himself.

"You can get more bees with honey than vinegar," Aretha had told him after the first encounter. He came from the captain's office heated, ready to throw his badge across the room. Aretha dragged him to the coffee shop next door to cool him off.

"So, how are things at home?" she'd started in.

"Home?" he asked, trying to get his mind back to her conversation. "Home? You mean—"

"Home. Charla. Your girlfriend and all that."

"Oh. Oh yeah, uh, it's all good," he'd lied. Things with him and Charla were far from good, but then again he couldn't do anything about that, either. He'd made a mess of relationships over the last few years—his and his parents', Phoebe, so why not just mess it all the way up with Charla. He'd cheated on her with Lacy, so things would never be "good at home" again. Hell, and what had he done but blow it with Lacy by sending her flowers after breaking her heart and then never calling her again.

Smooth move, Marcel!

But he'd learned to be a little smoother since then. He'd learned that talking to the captain required the utmost of smooth.

"You know how much red tape those guys gotta get through, Cap'n. . . ."

"Umhmm."

"Just let me keep at it, okay? Let me keep at it until they close their reports."

"We got that insurance guy breathing down our backs and—"

"Let me talk to him. Let me talk to him, and . . . and let me keep at it until he's the last one to deal with."

The captain looked at his desk calendar, still without looking up at Marcel. "The insurance guy said he wanted this thing resolved in a hundred and twenty days, and that's only because that brother-in-law of yours is suing that Durham woman."

"He's what?"

"He's suing her for the insurance money. So that's another mess. But it doesn't concern us. But, needless to say, if we haven't determined her death accidental we stand in the way of that little legal mess and I don't want that."

"So we need to determine her death an accident, or . . ." Marcel paused.

"Or not," the captain added, still not looking at Marcel.

"Within ninety days?"

"Within ninety days."

Marcel took that as a green light. The captain all but said he wasn't going to close the case for ninety days. That would be more than enough time to nail Harold for killing Phoebe. He knew it in his heart that Harold was dirty and he was going to prove it, even if it took a lifetime. He had ninety days, however, and that was going to have to be enough time.

He rushed back to his desk, ignoring Aretha's inquisitive expression. He picked up his phone and notepad. Flipping to the number of Steven Prophet, he knew he would continue where he'd left off in their last conversation. He all but had the green light now. Marcel also was sure that if this Steven guy was worth his salt he'd questioned people close to Phoebe's death. It was a shortcut, but he needed all the shortcuts he could get right now.

Chapter 18

Dave took the dogs on their daily walk along the cliffs. He had to admit he enjoyed their company. He wasn't lonely; as a matter of fact he knew too many people . . . All the time, people coming over, parties and loud living. He'd often contemplated spreading a rumor that he'd died, just to slow things down, especially after meeting *her*. During the week she was there, hiding her from his friends had become almost impossible. She, once she started feeling better after such a terrible bump on the head, sort of got into the charade and would change her name depending on who asked. It was as if she was meant to perform and was good at it . . . in the bed and out.

But, in all truthfulness, Dave envied Lacy's quiet life. She was an actress . . . of sorts, yet had managed to live privately. She had nobody clinging on just to glean her fame. She, her dogs, and her foulmouthed bird seemed very content to just *be*. Lacy was close to her parents and dedicated to her job. That's where she was now, at work.

Dave had the key to her house, and would stop in during the day to do a walkthrough (*as if anybody would come all the way out here to steal anything*), and walk her dogs. He laughed to himself at the thought of anyone coming all the way up here for mayhem, while glancing up the hill toward her house. The house was so secluded once he took the dogs for their walk, they would never take off toward home on their way back. It was as if they thought, *nobody home; why rush!* But today they did. They shot up the cliffs toward Lacy's house as he grew closer.

"Come back!" Dave called, rushing to keep up with them. "Where the hell are you going?" he called, rushing up the jagged rocks. "Nobody is there! She's not there!" he yelled. "She's at work, you silly nilly willies. . . ." he called after the dogs.

Reaching the top, he found them sitting in the yard, staring at the house. "You tryin' to kill me or what?" Dave continued to call toward them.

Just then the beautiful dark-haired mystery woman came from inside the house—relocking the door with what looked like a key. Dave's mouth dropped open before he could catch it. She was *au naturel,* as she was the day he found her unconscious on the rocks.

That night, he started to call 911, but she came to as he struggled with her body, trying to find a pulse.

"I need to get you some help," he told her.

"No! No!" she growled. Her face was fierce and her eyes like dark lava pools—intimidating, even against the fiery moon's light.

"Okay, okay, but I need to get you inside, where you can dry off, and out of this weather." At that Dave heard what sounded like an explosion off in the distance. He thought it was thunder. The woman, apparently hearing it too, paused as if contemplating things, and then nodded.

That was how it started. Dave took her into his home and nursed her concussion until she was better. They laughed together, ate together, and, within what seemed like moments, slept together, and Dave fell in love. He could only hope she did too.

Seeing her coming from Lacy's home, he was flabbergasted. The dogs must have been just as taken with her, as they did not threaten her with growls and snarls as they normally did to strangers.

"I would never try to kill anyone . . . on purpose," the woman said, smiling broadly.

"Hi. I'm sorry, what?"

"Oh, I heard you say that to the dogs and was just . . ." She sounded nervous, and was fumbling with what looked like a small pocket sized tool kit.

"Oh yes, right," Dave said. "Doing some work for Lacy? She need a repair or something?" he asked, pointing at the kit.

"No, I . . ."

He felt awkward. It was an awkward moment. "My name is David," he said, outstretching his hand as if meeting her for the first time.

Sliding her slender hand into his, she said after taking a deep sigh, "And I'm a horrible person who you really don't want to know."

"Nobody is home, but then I guess you know that," he said, noticing her holding the key to Lacy's house.

She looked down guiltily. "Yes, I . . . I saw that. I . . . Yes, I was fixing something that I broke last time I was here."

Noting that the dogs were quietly sitting—no barking, snarling, or otherwise—Dave was puzzled by the woman, again. "Look, I don't know who you are or what you want, but, crazy though it may sound, it's as if you belong here. I want to know how you know Lacy. I know she has friends . . . I guess, but nobody ever comes up here." Dave was laughing goofily now. He was excited and couldn't hide it. "Why has she never told me about you? I thought I knew everything about her. Why do you have a key? What're you doing here, for crying out loud? I want to know. I need to know."

"Dave, it's not safe for you to know. I can't explain anything. I have to go," she said, starting to leave.

Dave took her by the arm, stopping her. "Try. Start from the beginning. I have all day. I have the rest of my life."

The woman looked around nervously. Her beautiful dark eyes began to brim with water. Dave's heart nearly gave out. In his life he'd had many mysterious women cross his path . . . men too for that matter. He was very continental and worldly, but this woman, this woman touched him deeper than the flesh. He immediately trusted her; hell, the dogs even trusted her. She was changed somehow from the woman he took in a few weeks back, but there was one thing that was the same—her air of mystery. Dave wanted to know more about her. He was willing to play with fire on this one, and she looked as hot as they came. "Talk to me," he said.

"You don't understand. If I tell you, I may have to kill you." She chuckled.

"I'll take my chances. You look killer but you don't look like a killer to me."

The woman sighed heavily. "We went to school together, Lacy and I. I have always sort of . . . I can't explain it, but I needed to see her. I think she's in danger and it's all my fault. I needed to tell her," the woman began.

Chapter 19

That night, while trying to enjoy a little TV, Lacy found herself fidgeting. The movie had gotten intense, too. Lacy actually clicked the off button on her DVD player and sat, pondering the plot.

What if . . .

She began pondering writing a story about something just as bizarre as the movie she had been trying to watch. Just then, there was a knock on her front door. Harriet and Oz almost went into convulsions. They acted as if no one had ever knocked on her door before. But, then again, it wasn't often and never this late at night. She approached it slowly. "Who is it?" she barked, trying to sound as tough as the dogs.

"The police, ma'am!" a voice called back sternly.

The voice was one that sounded like a voice she had heard somewhere before, but she couldn't place it.

"The police? What do you want?"

"I'm here to question a tall, skinny lady with long legs . . . about a dog."

"Pardon me?"

"It's me, legs."

"Gary?"

"Yeah."

She looked down at her dogs, knowing they would have him for a late-night snack given the chance. "Hold on," she said, rushing them into their little room off the kitchen. She hurried back to the door, still not sure about whether to let him in, but just in case she did there was no reason for him to be eaten alive . . . *right?*

"You bastard," she heard nasty Pete say.

Pete can cuss at him. That would be okay, she thought. Lacy turned to Pete and pretended to scold the smart bird by playfully shaking his cage. He screamed at the discipline and it made her laugh. "What do you want, Gary?" she called through the heavy oak door, still not sure she wanted to let him in.

"It's freezing, legs. Open the door so we can talk. Come on, we need to talk," he begged. "We've played the break-up game long enough." Opening the door slightly, Lacy was caught off guard to find a red-nosed, fully inebriated Gary. He pushed past her into the middle of the living room. "So, let's see what other little gifts and things you've gotten from your little copper boyfriend, bitch," he spat.

"You bastard!" Pete squawked.

Spinning himself around, he leaned forward into the cage "And you stink," he growled at the bird.

Lacy reached for his arm to stop him from entering any farther. With the motion her robe opened slightly. He noticed her exposed breast.

"Working?" he asked.

"No, Gary, sleeping. You need to go."

"Ohhh, other men can come here but not me. I have to sneak around with you, huh?"

"Gary, that was your choice, but I don't want to go into it," she said, starting for the door to open it for his exit. "And what other men? Nobody comes here."

"I've seen them come here. I've followed them here. They come here." He moved up close to her face. He inhaled her scent. Lacy, only for a second, wondered if he could smell Marcel on her body. She pushed him back.

"Get out, Gary. Leave!"

Instead of leaving, he grabbed a handful of her curls and slapped her face hard. Pulling away from him, she ran for the dog's door, with him right on her heels in angry attack. She began to scream loudly as he tackled her to the floor as she entered the kitchen. He punched her between the shoulders before rolling her over and pulling open her robe. Sitting on her, he began to un-buckle his pants. She swung upward at him as hard as she could before reaching up and digging her nails deep into his face. In his drunken state, he rolled off of her, holding his face, yelling violent obscenities at her. She scrambled to her feet, finally reaching the doggie door. Opening it, she found that Oz and Harriet were waiting to protect her, eagerly.

Lacy called the dogs off only after Gary's screams became too much and there was a little blood. In the meantime, she dug through her kitchen catch-all drawer for the gun her father had given her. Holding the loaded .22-caliber pointed at him, she called the police. They came without much delay.

One of the officers was a petite blond woman. Though her blue eyes were soft, behind that heavy badge she was very serious. Her badge read "C. Thomas," and, for a second, as they hauled mangled, mauled, and be-ginning-to-sober-up Gary Jones from her living room, Lacy thought about Marcel's lady. She was a cop.

What irony, she thought. The wicked thought made Lacy smile. What if this was . . .

"I got him in the car, Charla," the male cop said. Lacy's heart tightened.

"Are you going to be all right?" Charla asked as she handed Lacy back her gun. She had run the routine check to make sure Lacy was legally armed. She was licensed to carry the gun. Again her father had made sure all her t's were crossed and i's dotted. She kept another gun in her car in a locked box in her trunk for security. It was a .45-caliber that her father had bought her when she left for college. He made sure his little girl was very safe.

"Can't be too sure when you're on your own out here in the city," he said.

"Oh, yeah, Daddy. I get beat up every day," Lacy *retorted, sounding smart-alecky.*

"You've got quite a shiner there. Are you sure you don't want to press charges?" Charla asked again, bringing Lacy back with the repeat of the question.

Lacy looked past her to the car where Gary sat looking pitiful and full of remorse in the back seat. She was bundled in her heavy throw now, standing in the cold. She shook her head, knowing that he would be regretting this enough in the morning.

As the officers drove off, Lacy was torn with all the emotions she felt. Guilt, vindication, validation, and more guilt consumed her. She looked down at the card Charla had handed her. It read "Marcel DuChamp." "God, she musta grabbed up the wrong cards from his side of the bed," Lacy said, feeling her stomach start to turn. She rushed to the bathroom to throw up.

Chapter 20

"I thought I'd have my money by now," the big man growled. "It's been way over thirty days." He'd busted in the door as if he had an invitation.

The tall woman looked furious. She had to admit she was a little terrified, but refused to let it show. "I said we're working on it," she explained. "Shit happens."

"Well, you bitches aren't working fast enough! The only shit that's happened is that my boat is gone. My livelihood is on hold because of you bitches," he went on, pointing at the tall woman and the other woman involved with this scheme . . . *The scheme that damned lawyer Adam Stillberg said would work but hasn't as of yet,* Barry Nugent realized.

"It takes time," the tall woman said, repeating what sounded like lines she was reciting from a script. She glared at the other woman as if she had unfinished business with her.

"Listen, you fat fuck, you just better wait," the other woman blurted, stepping out of the line of the taller woman's glare. She was showing a little spunk. The man turned to her, grabbed her around the throat, and slammed her against the wall.

"Shit!" the tall woman exploded now, immediately reaching for a weapon. The woman being choked gasped for air while telling everyone to calm down, but it was too late.

Blam!

The bat made contact with the back of the big man's head. Not once but three times the tall woman hit him, harder with each blow, until the man released the woman and fell to the floor shaking, jerking, and then closing his eyes. He was dead. She hit him one more time for good measure, though.

"Shit! Now what do we do?" the choking woman gasped, coughing slightly while stepping closer. She looked around the floor at the sprayed blood. "He's huge; what do we do now?"

"We move him. We dump his fat ass in the ocean right by the boathouse where we found him," the tall woman said.

"Oh my God! This is getting out of hand. Nobody was supposed to get killed," the woman who had gotten choked said, rubbing her throat, feeling the scratches.

"Please! You knew this could happen. You act like this is all some bad movie script. People are going to die! Get that through your fuckin' head," the tall woman with the bat told her. She sounded cold and filled with something other than feminine feelings. "You wimping out? You fuckin' wimpin' out?" she screamed at the woman rubbing her neck.

"No! No!" the woman said, sounding panicked now and growing fearful.

"Good, because this is not the end of it! This is the start, baby!"

Hearts were pounding. The air was thick. At first this had seemed easy; they'd had a plan. The boat. The insurance money. It was supposed to all look like an accident. But no, Harold had messed everything up by not getting on the boat in time. He was supposed to be dead; Phoebe was supposed to get off the boat. She was supposed to collect off his policy and this was supposed to be over.

Naming Lacy was a joke, something Phoebe decided while drunk one night after a filming. She hated Harold, and so naming Queen Hynata, the man hater, as beneficiary to a bogus insurance claim seemed harmless enough. Besides, she remembered the childhood promise they had made to each other. The promise made to will each other all their earthly possessions. She also remembered that Lacy had indeed named her in her will. So when plans changed and Phoebe ended up "dead," those two things began to cog together into a plan—a plan that couldn't have been better if planned. But now people are getting second thoughts. They are getting demanding. They are turning what should be a simple thing into a biggo fat mess, the taller woman, Sonja, thought, looking at the big dead man lying in the middle of her floor.

"Dammit!" She stomped. "And trust me. This is just a first casualty. There will be more. So get ready for it if this shit takes much longer. I'm sick of waiting for my money!" She pointed the bloody bat at her partner. "Now stop staring and help me get him up."

Chapter 21

The bright morning sun coming through her window woke her up. Lacy realized how stiff she felt as she tried to climb out of bed. Her pets seemed drugged too. Not one of them was jumping about, eager to start the day. She felt as if all of them had been somewhere and just gotten back. She, for one, felt exhausted. The swelling on her face was obvious and the mirror confirmed the black eye. There would be no going into work today. She didn't know if the police had taken Gary in to sleep it off or let him go, considering she hadn't pressed charges. Either way, work was not where she wanted to be after a night like last night. In her mind, they knew. She'd walk in and somehow everyone there would know everything, and she just wasn't in the mood for it.

She dressed and headed for the kitchen for some coffee. The thought of it turned her stomach. She needed to get out.

A walk along the cliffs with the dogs cleared her head considerably. She hadn't taken her dogs out for a walk in quite a while. The ocean was a clear blue and very still as she covered a good solid mile before tiring.

"Did you fall?" Dave asked, calling to her as she topped the cliff at his deck to water her dogs. It was customary for them to invade each other's space this way without notice. She had to realize that maybe she and Dave were closer than either of them ever really addressed.

"No, I got into a fight." She laughed.

His eyes widened as he proceeded to enjoy a good belly laugh on that one as well. He laughed so hard he almost fell off his deck swing, as he imagined Lacy's slender frame up against the likes of a Mike Tyson type. She could tell he was picturing her as Queen Hynata at that moment, which actually she found a little bit funny too—considering.

"No, I . . ." She paused. "I guess I officially broke up with Gary."

"Broke up what? You and Gary weren't anything," Dave said, coming over and petting the dogs that now looked around as if sensing something of interest. The female, Harriet, took off inside Dave's house through the patio door. Both Lacy and Dave watched her run off, and then looked at each other. Dave shrugged. "What's that about?"

"She's so crazy," Lacy said about her dog, hoping Dave wouldn't come back to the conversation they had started. Of course he did.

"He hit you?" Dave reached to touch the bruised area but Lacy flinched.

"Yeah. He was drunk. I called the cops and . . ." Lacy thought about Charla. Her chest tightened. "They came."

"Boy, there's nothing going on and then suddenly this hill becomes a busy place," Dave said, looking around with a forlorn sigh escaping his lips.

"Yeah, mystery women and boxing ex-boyfriends, what's next?" She playfully hit his shoulder. "Oh yeah, and by the way, did the people ever come out to fix, like, my air ducts or whatever? They were from the mortgage company."

He jumped as if he had truly mentally exited their space for a moment but the question had brought him back. They both were obviously preoccupied with things unsaid, of that Lacy was sure.

"Yes! Yes, they were here and took care of everything," he answered quickly.

Lacy noted his nervous tone but didn't say anything. "Coolio. Look, I'm going to my folks' in a couple of weeks for Thanksgiving. Are we good with our usual arrangement? I mean, I feel as though I should ask," Lacy finally said after they both shared a moment on their own planets.

Dave looked back toward his house and then at her. "Yeah, yeah, sure. You never have to ask me anything, Lacy. I'm your friend. I care about you. A lot of people do."

"Dave, what's going on?"

"Nothing. I'm just saying, I think you should go to your parents'. I think you should see some old friends." He nodded, as if satisfied with his own words.

"Yeah," Lacy agreed, in a probing way. "Going to my parents' is always good. Don't know about that old friend thing but . . ." She was thinking about the last time she'd seen an old friend. Her eyes began to burn at the thought of Marcel. The sound of his moaning replayed loudly in her ears. She shook her head to shut it out.

"Yeah, yeah," he said again, glancing back toward his house. "Especially with that creep Gary and all."

"Gary isn't going to be a problem. I'm more worried about the Martians."

"Yeah," Dave agreed, sounding mindless and distracted by what may have been going on in his house.

Lacy then decided to step over the invisible boundaries they had drawn in their friendship. "I'ma go get the dog," she said, storming into his house.

"Wait!" Dave yelped, racing behind her.

Inside Dave's house there was an obviously new feel. Many of his painting tools were out and it looked as if he'd started on a portrait of a woman. Lacy tried to make her out from the rough sketch, but she just looked like chalk lines without a true definition or identification—it was just a raceless, faceless frontal etching of a nude woman.

"Why, Dave, you've been entertaining?" she asked with a smile.

He grinned nervously. "She came back."

"Oh my God! When? Why didn't you tell me?"

"I didn't want to jinx anything. I mean, she didn't stay long, but she promised she'd be back again. She just came for a little while and . . . and . . ." He blushed slightly. "It was wonderful, Lacy. I started a painting of her. I was scared Harriet was going to damage this when she came in here, and that's why I panicked. Anyway"—Dave sighed heavily—"I'm in love with her."

"Do you know her name?" Lacy asked, sounding tongue-in-cheek.

"Of course, you knucklehead. Raven. Her name is Raven."

"Oooooh, sounds sexy," Lacy teased, nudging him goofily with her hip.

He looked down at where their bodies bumped. "What the hell is that?" he asked, pointing at her hip area.

"What?"

"That tub of lard you just hit me with!"

"Dave! Oh my God," Lacy yelped, wrapping her windbreaker tighter around her body. "I've put on a little weight. Okay, so I've been a little depressed and the only thing handy is Chinese food and chocolate."

"Honey, the closest Chinese is down this hill. That is hardly handy." Dave was laughing now.

"Okay, okay, so midnight runs included. I'm leaving! Harriet!" She called her dog, who now came bounding from where she had made herself comfortable. The male dog stood obediently by her side. "I hope you're not this rude to your new lady friend. My God!" Lacy pouted before storming out.

Dave was still laughing.

When Lacy left, Dave gave his etching a closer look. With all the gentleness of a feather he felt the woman's hands run up his back.

"I can't believe you said Lacy was getting fat," the woman he knew only as Raven whispered in his ear.

"Oh please, you should have seen her. She looks like Miss Piggy—all swollen in the face and puffy. She's turned into a buttercup." Dave avoided telling her about Lacy's incident with Gary and kissed her instead, before, with a loving gaze, they read each other's need and slowly drifted back to Dave's bedroom.

Lacy, on the other hand, sulked and cried on the sofa with a bag of dried tropical fruit chunks.

Before long her father called to ask her how the book was coming along. Knowing she was blocked and had been for months made her cry even more. She couldn't stop crying and talking until she had told him finally about Gary and what had happened. She then told him about Marcel.

"Well," was all he said, after clearly getting an earful of her soupy, soggy saga. "The boy next door. It's always the boy next door."

"I'm sorry, Daddy. I'm sorry I'm failing at this thing called life."

"You're not failing. Get a grip, you're sounding like your mother. Stop being so dramatic. You only have so many options. You can run home and hide under the bed. I can come get you and bring you home to hide under the bed. You can accept that we sold your bed a few years ago and stay at your own house under your own bed, or . . ." By then he was snickering.

Lacy loved hearing her father's laughter. It told her that everything would be all right. He'd raised her to be independent and strong. At the moment, she had to accept that, for some reason, she was just having a hard time putting it into practice. But, after tonight, she was no longer going to just let things happen by chance. She was in control of her life.

Lacy decided to get over Marcel and her childish crush, along with Gary and his taking her for cheap and unappreciated. She was going to visit her parents for Thanksgiving in a couple of weeks and everything was going to be fine.

Yeah, right—nothing is fine, she thought, thinking about how far from okay everything really was right now.

Chapter 22

Marcel couldn't sleep. It was the start of the holiday season. His ulcer had been acting up again. It had been doing that since before Halloween, so he figured that must have been what was causing his insomnia.

He had a head full of thoughts as he paced his apartment floor. He had talked with Denise about his unending suspicions about Harold and everything surrounding Phoebe's death. She was a bevy of information. She'd been calling him nonstop, so he finally took her up on a lunch date, and she was like a volcano eruption of gossip and hearsay. He constantly asked her, "How do you know that?" only to be ignored, until finally he just listened.

Apparently, Denise prided herself on her powers of deduction. He was used to this talent, having partnered with Aretha for so long. He thought Aretha had ESP until he realized that most answers are right in front of us, but we as people usually over think the obvious or rely on happenstance to move things forward. People like Aretha and Denise relied on something different.

"You see, Marcel, people put their own destiny in motion by assuming that someone else is trying to change it. For instance, Phoebe wanted something"— Denise smiled coquettishly—"or someone, and she felt that someone else, let's just say Lacy, was trying to take that from her. She unconsciously put things in motion and so on and so on until you and Lacy ended up in bed together, which is the one thing that Phoebe didn't want!"

"What?" Marcel yelped, wondering where this direction of conversation came from.

"Oh, did I hit a nerve?"

"Denise, you are off track. Get back on track."

Denise grinned. "I know about the sleepover. Winston was not as asleep as you guys thought. Annnnnyway."

"Oh."

"Oh yeah, anyway, but there is one thing that puzzles me," Denise said, obviously getting ready to switch gears or dig deeper; either way, Marcel was ready for her. "I know it's probably just my wild imagination, as my husband calls it, but why would Sonja miss the funeral when she was supposedly Phoebe's best friend and she's right here in town?"

"Sonja is in town?"

"Marcel, she's the one who called me to tell me Phoebe was dead."

"You didn't tell me that."

"You didn't ask me."

"Denise, do you know if Harold and Sonja are still seeing each other? I'm not stupid. I know they had a . . . a thing," Marcel said, admitting what he always tried to avoid thinking about. It was back right after Phoebe and Harold got married. Sonja had come into the States for a photo shoot, Phoebe had said. But when he saw Harold and Sonja together he didn't see any cameras. What he saw looked like an intimate, romantic dinner, so Marcel just went with it.

"Harold and Sonja weren't having an affair."

"Really?"

"Marcel . . . Phoebe and Sonja were. I thought you knew. I thought Lacy knew too, I teased her about

Phoebe and her lover at the funeral and she didn't get it either."

"What?"

"Let me stop right here. Just let me stop." She glanced at her watch. "Not to tell you how to do your job, but you need to rent more porn," she said flatly.

"What?"

"Talk to you later, Marcel," Denise said before quickly gathering her things and strutting off.

At first Marcel took what she said as confusing and worth only being put out of his mind; that is, until he visited with the harbormaster about the boat that went up the night Phoebe was pronounced dead at sea.

"Can I speak with the person who owned the boat at least?"

"Nope. He's moved on. Man, you don't keep up. He lost his boat in that biggo fire and shit. It was tragic. Barry was a good guy."

"Moved on? Do you know where?"

"I heard rumors."

"What kind of rumors?"

"Well, I mean, I don't wanna go to the police station or anything like that. I mean, I'm a busy man and what's done is done."

"Right. Right. I'm off duty. I'm just here as a brother who lost his sister in that tragic accident. When Barry's boat went up, my sister went down. She died on that boat."

"Gottdamn, I'm sorry," the man said, shaking his head sadly. "I just heard some porn queen died in the fire . . ." The harbormaster's face grew beet red. Marcel held tight to his emotions. "Fuck me. I'm sorry, man, was that your sister?"

"So, um . . . yeah, I'm just here asking some questions, uh, yeah, about my, uhhh, sister. Ya know, I'm just wanting ta know some stuff. I mean, I need to tell our mom and dad some new stuff about what happened here that night."

"I hear ya, Mac . . . And, well, I'm sure you want to have some peace and something good to tell Mom and Dad, I'm sure. I never thought about the family of a gal like that . . . you know."

"Yeah, uh, anyway, can you fill me in on what happened that night? Were you there?"

"Nah, but Barry come in one day, hot as a firecracker about his boat, right? He says to me damn bitches got him all tangled up in a mess. Says all he'd done was rent his boat to this film crew, ya know? Sure, he knew they were gonna film some porn but what the hell, right? A buck is a buck. Now, he says, now his insurance company is gonna investigate the possibility of him blowing up his own boat. That's chicken shit, I say. He wasn't even on the boat. You know, those type of filming crews don't like people around, dig?"

"So this is after?" Marcel asked, still trying to stay impartial.

The guy nodded. "I'm like, what the hell, Barry, you weren't nowheres near your boat when it happened. He'd rented it out, you know"—he pointed at Marcel— "to your purdy little sister and that brother-in-law of yours and some other guy . . . Attorney, yeah, that's what Barry said he was. Said they had brought their own attorney—sounds like kinky shit to me. I can see the title now, *Sex and the Man in the Lawyer Suit*," the guy said as if making a marquee. He snickered before realizing again he was speaking not only with a police officer, but to the brother of the porn actress making the film.

"Okay, and then he said . . . ?"

The man cleared his throat. "Well that's all he says, really, and that now his money is being held up and that some bitches got him all messed up now."

"Bitches, huh?" Marcel pondered the plural of the word. "He didn't say who the bitches were, or why it was their fault he wasn't getting his money?"

The man shook his head vehemently. "Nope, and then the next day he's gone so we'll never know now, will we?"

You may not, Marcel thought. *But nobody just disappears . . . Not Barry . . . not Phoebe. Not Phoebe's secrets. Everybody and everything shows up somewhere sooner or later.*

Marcel wondered if Lacy knew about Phoebe's occupation. If not, he wondered how she and he had managed to be the only people left on earth left in the dark. As much as he hated to do it, he needed to keep his eye on Lacy a bit longer from the shadows of her life before interacting. He had things to ask her, but he worried about how far they'd get face to face. Maybe he was just a coward, but there were just a few too many things he was finding hard to accept. He needed to get away—go see his folks. He was actually pretty excited about the visit home. It'd been way too long.

Chapter 23

Finally, vacation day had come. Lacy reached her parents' home. She felt excited. The thought of eating thrilled her to no end. She was depressed, stressed, and ready to throw in the towel and then throw up on it. She hadn't told her mother how sick she'd been feeling because she didn't want to chance being told to stay home. She hadn't had a fever, and nobody at work had called in sick so she couldn't say she was contagious. She just knew she felt like crap. She hated the thought of making her parents sick, but she just really needed to spend the next five days with them.

Dave seemed a bit excited too. She'd never seen him so giddy and boyish. Maybe he was planning a huge party or something. It had been awhile since he'd entertained. When she first moved on the hill Dave was a party animal, but after last Christmas it just seemed all his friends started getting "too busy." Lacy could relate. But, then again, Dave was a bit of a downer last year at this time, but since the first of the year his spirits had seemed to lift a little each month. He would always say he owed it to a special friend who'd dropped into his life unexpectedly. She knew he meant her but she never wanted the burden of the weight of that kind of friendship. Besides, she was on a major downer herself lately.

"I swear if Pete doesn't stop cussing he's gonna end up on the Thanksgiving table," Dave threatened after Pete cursed him bitterly.

"Don't even joke about it!" Lacy screeched.

"I hate you!" Pete concurred. "I love you," he finally said. Lacy was shocked. She'd been trying to get him to say that for months. Dave burst into laughter; more laughter than the situation called for, in Lacy's opinion. But everybody deserved to be happy.

She'd asked to see his painting but he refused. Lacy had to wonder what the biggo secret was.

Opening her trunk, her mind came back to where she was—at her parents' home. Glancing over at Marcel's parents' house, she noticed the driveway was empty. She felt sad. This holiday was one when she counted on seeing Phoebe. She thought about the last Thanksgiving. Harold was being such a jerk. He'd gotten drunk and treated Phoebe like shit. He kept calling her a queen and taunting her about not making it to television the way Lacy had. He'd only done it because Marcel hadn't come. At the time she hadn't known, but now she got it: apparently last year Marcel had decided to spend the holiday with . . .

Lacy's eyes began to burn.

Charla.

"Sweetheart!" her mother called, rushing from the house as if she'd not been in months instead of weeks. Halloween had just been a few weeks before. She'd only spent the night to help hand out candy, but still.

Stepping out of the car, she squeezed her mother tight, only to have her mother step back from her. "My God you're getting fat."

"Thanks," Lacy answered. Her mood lowered even more.

Just then, Lacy noticed the sedan pulling into the driveway next door. "Oh, how sweet," her mother said while sighing and holding her chest dramatically. She looked like a TV mom. "Marcelly is spending the holiday with his mother. I'm so happy for her. We'll have to have them over later, after their meal. I was debating having the block over for dessert. Marcelly showing up cinches it. "

"No. I don't think . . ." Lacy began to explain before her mother headed into the house, totally ignoring her.

Chapter 24

Dinner was quiet for the three of them: Lacy and her parents. Lacy tried to control herself but the food was just way too good.

"Lacy, honey, are you eating?" her mother finally said, noticing her third round of potatoes.

"Sarah, let the girl eat. You know she's always had a good appetite."

"I know, Ray, but a young girl her age only eats like this when she's given up on love—or love's given up on her."

"Mom, what's love gotta do . . ." Lacy joked, filling her mouth with a forkful of turkey/potato mix. "Yum," she then said.

Her father smiled at her. "My baby can have anybody she wants. You want anybody, sweetie?" he asked. Lacy shook her head vehemently. "There," he said.

Sarah wasn't buying it. She started at Lacy hard and then took a small nibble. "So your job is going well?"

"Yes," Lacy answered.

"And your sex life?"

Ray choked on his tea. Lacy jumped up and began patting his back heartily. "Mother!" she screeched.

"I'm just concerned about your health. You look tired and so I figured you weren't getting enough vitamin 'P.'"

Ray continued to choke.

Later that night, after dinner, Lacy held a tight smile as the DuChamps entered the house: Marcel and his parents. Lacy hugged the older couple. Marcel and she froze before Marcel gave her a quick hug and peck on the cheek. Marcel's mother noticed and hunched Marcel's father, who was the normal voice in the family.

"Oh, please, you act like you hate girls Marcel. Give Lacy a real hug. It's been a long time since you've seen each other. I promise I won't tell your girlfriend. You know, the girl I've never met," Marcel's father teased, pushing Marcel into Lacy for a real hug.

Marcel hugged her again. Their eyes met. Slowly he attempted to kiss her, but she turned her lips away just in time to catch it on the cheek.

"Marcel!" Mrs. Potter yelled out. She was excited to see him. "Oh it's been so long, and look, my Susie is all grown up," she said, pointing at her daughter, who frowned at the thought of her mother playing match-maker this way. Susie was older than Lacy and Marcel by two years.

"Mrs. Potter, Susie's been married already, if any-body deserves a shot, it's Lacy here. Surely she's gonna be a spinster if we don't get her married off here soon! How old are you now, honey?" Mr. Jones asked. Lacy's face felt hot. Susie couldn't help but cover her face—embarrassed for the both of them.

"Spinster?" Marcel whispered.

"Shut up," she whispered back.

"Don't you have a girlfriend?" Lacy's mother asked Marcel, who started to answer but was interrupted by his mother.

"Who knows? Frankly I don't believe she's real. I've never met her. Who has?" Marcel's mother spoke up surprisingly. She was joined by all the other mothers in the room in letting out a healthy sigh.

"She's real, Mrs. DuChamp, and she's lovely. I ran into Marcel and Charla . . ." Lacy began, placing special emphasis on Charla's name.

"Charla," everyone chimed in as if the name were magical and being heard for the first time. Marcel groaned. Susie chuckled again. It seemed like Susie, Lacy, Marcel, and Bill were the only "children" of the neighborhood who had shown up this year. Of course, Bill had never left so it wasn't sure if he counted.

"I ran into them in the city. They were having lunch," Lacy went on.

"Oh yeah, that was the day I thought you were having lunch with someone too, but no, you had ordered all that food for yourself," Marcel said aloud.

Bill snickered while he poured himself some punch. "You two are a hoot. Do you see each other often in the city?" he asked them.

"No!" they both answered at the same time.

"Lacy and I don't run in the same circle. Besides, I watch grown-up TV and, you know, Lacy's into cartoons," Marcel dug.

"Actually, Charla and Marcel, they are a gorgeous couple, despite the fact that she's taller than Marcel too," Lacy dug back before picking up a dessert tray of ladyfingers and offering them to Marcel. "Here, have the finger in the middle," she whispered.

"Oh no, saving that one for you," he whispered back.

"Lacy, why are you gaining so much weight?" Mrs. Jones blurted then, sliding a cookie off the tray. "You should get a boyfriend before doing that," she said.

"I think she's beautiful," Bill sighed, wearing a red Kool-Aid moustache. Marcel stared at him and then at Lacy. He couldn't help but burst into laughter and walk away.

Chapter 25

Detective Lawrence Miller arrived on the scene a little later than his partner, Jim Beem. He'd been out visiting his mother at the assisted living complex where she lived now. She was a feisty woman who demanded a lot of his attention, especially when cussing at the staff on a daily basis. Tonight being a holiday had made it especially challenging for the staff and Lawrence. And now he had to work. He hoped it was going to be something easy, but when he arrived Jim's face said it all.

"Nasty," Jim said. "Been here a minute."

"Ugh," Lawrence said, peeking over the shoulder of a photographer and wrinkling his nose again.

"No ID, but the guy who found him said his name was Barry and he was pretty well known around here."

"Known as what? Fish bait?"

"Ha! Good one, Lawrence. I love your mood after a visit with your mother—"

"That's Hell Mother to you," Lawrence began.

"Was she fightin' again?"

"Of course," Lawrence said, approaching the man who had called in. "Hey, you call this in?"

"Yeah. I was coming down to do a little fishing and, well, I found him here on the rocks. Looks like he might have washed up. We all around here had thought he moved away. Nobody has seen him for a long time."

"And you know this is him because . . . ?" Jim said, noticing that the puffy, bloated remains had to look very little like who he once was.

"He always wore that jacket." The man who called in pointed at what was left of Barry Nugent's Oakland A's jacket.

"Ahhh." Both men nodded.

Jim turned to an empty page on his tablet. "And you are . . . ?"

"Mark. Mark Bower."

"You know him well, Mark?"

"Yeah, everybody did—like I told you earlier." He looked at Lawrence, who just stood, listening. It was clear Mark hoped Jim wasn't going to make him repeat his story just because Lawrence had come late. "He was popular. He lost his boat a few months back. He got kinda depressed. I think he was having some money problems."

"Depressed?" Jim asked. Lawrence quickly noticed the indention in what was left of Barry's head. The rest of him looked intact—for a waterlogged corpse. Then Jim noticed what looked like a bullet hole between the eyes. He'd not killed himself unless he'd run into wall a few times and then shot himself between the eyes while unconscious, or the other way around.

"Kept saying something about insurance and all that—we all thought he just sorta . . . you know, went away, maybe like to work it out or whatever."

"He have many friends, enemies, family?"

"Yeah, all the above . . . Popular guy."

"Okay, well we'll see about missing persons and all that but, let me ask you, when's the last time you saw him?"

"It was a little bit ago. Like I said, he was bellyaching about money and how he was waiting on some for a job he did. He'd been drinking so I'm sure he didn't mean what he was sayin'," Mark began, sounding as if he didn't want to finish his sentence.

"What was he sayin'?"

"He was saying that he shoulda known better than to do what he'd done."

"What had he done?"

Mark looked around, and then back at Jim and Lawrence. "Well, it sounded like he was saying he'd killed someone. But I . . . I'm not sure." Mark hesitated.

Lawrence interjected, "Wow, and you didn't try to get that clearly understood?"

"No! I don't need that kind of trouble. I'm just sayin' what I thought I heard him sayin'!"

Jim attempted to calm the situation by speaking in a low tone. "That's fair, Mark. That's fair. So you think he may have killed himself?"

Mark, too, looked at the body. It didn't take a forensic expert to tell Barry's wounds were probably not self-inflicted. "I can't say," Mark answered safely. "I can't say anything except that here he is, boys. Now do your job."

"That's fair, Mark Bowers, so with that said, we may need to question you a little further on this," Jim said, holding up a large bag of marijuana found in Mark Bower's possession.

"Yeah, I figured as much," Mark said, sounding disgusted and slightly disappointed.

Chapter 26

Lacy held back her voice with all her might as Marcel's pace increased. They were like animals unable to control the passion.

The tension had been building over the last two hours they'd spent slamming and insulting each other to reduce suspicion that maybe something between them had happened. The last thing they needed was their pushy parents forcing purpose into what was just an accident. Finally, a simple trip out to the trash had given them too much time together alone.

"Taller than me?" he had asked.

Lacy giggled in response. "Fat!"

"Well you are, kinda," he teased, tossing the large bag into the Dumpster, and then, instead of taking her bag, he grabbed her butt. Tossing her bag in, she turned to swat his hand and it landed on her breasts, her face, her lips. Pulling her into him by the back of her head, they kissed hungrily, tasting the ladyfingers, chocolate cake, and ice cream they'd eaten like children at her parents' cocktail table.

Slowly licking frosting off cupcakes while watching each other from across the room, the seduction began. By the time it was cleanup time, both were eager to volunteer for trash detail—together—hoping no one noticed.

Marcel lifted Lacy's leg high around his waist, pulling her onto his ready member. "I see you wore a skirt. Who were you trying to catch, Bill?"

On Marcel's signal, she'd eased out from the guests earlier on one of her many trips to the bathroom to remove her panties. It wasn't so much what he'd said as what he did that made her know what he had planned. She was mixing up some Chex Mix for the card-playing men when Marcel walked past and reached for a glass in the cabinet; it was how he did it that let her know. He reached over her backside, allowing himself to press against her. He was hard as stone, she could tell.

Now that rod was ramming through her as they stood against the fence. "Oh yeah, Bill . . . umhmmm definitely," Lacy said vampishly, grunting and sounding primal and earthy as he entered her without further hesitation.

"Damn, you feel so good, Lace," he said in her ear. She couldn't say anything, for fear she would squeal too loudly instead. "I want you. I want you," he purred.

"I . . . I . . . I lo—" Lacy attempted to speak but suddenly and unexpectedly he came.

"Shit," he gasped before pulling free from her hurriedly. Lacy accepted the quickie for what it was and smoothed down her skirt. It was just in time, too.

"Hey, you kids, hurry back in. We're gonna play another game! The Montgomerys left and we need you two to fill in," Lacy's mother called.

"Okay, Mother," Lacy called. Her voice was notably shaky.

Her mother clearly noticed. "You okay?"

"We're fine, Mrs. Durham," Marcel answered. "Lacy saw a worm," he added. With that comment, Lacy burst into giggles.

All eyes were on them as they reentered the house, except for the eyes of their own parents. Lacy found the phenomenon amazing. "Lacy, since you and Marcel are heel draggers you guys have to play on the same team.

Now, please, try to get along," Lacy's mother said, avoiding eye contact.

"We will, Mrs. Durham," Marcel answered quickly.

"You're such a good boy," she said, refusing to look at Marcel.

"I bet he's great," Susie all but growled, catching Lacy up in a gaze that caused Lacy to grow uncomfortable.

"I'll be right back," Lacy said then, dashing into the bathroom. Shutting the door behind her, she couldn't stop giggling.

When she came out of the bathroom, Marcel was gone.

"He got a call. He's a good cop. He had to go," Marcel's father said before Lacy could ask. "So we changed games. You'll be my partner, 'kay?"

Lacy tried not to allow her instant deflating to show. "Oh, of course. That's better anyhow. . . ."

Chapter 27

"Well, I am of the mind to fight Mr. Kitchener on this matter and side with Ms. Durham on the money," Steven Prophet said, sounding forceful and determined.

"What? She's not next of kin. She's not the surviving spouse. That's crazy," Adam Stillberg barked. "Besides, Mr. Kitchener has a right to protect his investments. Like it or not, he was Mrs. Kitchener's manager, and I as their attorney advised him to protect his investment this way."

This was the first time Steven had actually taken a meeting face to face with this Adam guy, but he was pretty tired of him already. Steven had gotten tired of playing phone tag with him and just finally called and set up an appointment. He wanted to verify his thoughts on Adam Stillberg. *Yep, he is a slime ball,* Steven internally summed up.

"A wife is not an investment.

"A future porn star is though . . . and that's what Phoebe DuChamp was turning into. Had the accident not happened, the film they were making had all the makings of the next *Deep Throat*. It was destined to be a classic."

"You're sick—"

"And you'll lose. You'll just waste time and money that"—Adam made a gesture in the air that Steven could see was purely filled with sarcasm—"Queen Hynata doesn't have and has no rights to."

"Yeah, but she's a cartoon. Lacy Durham is the beneficiary." Steven moved a photo that sat on Adam Stillberg's desk. It was a nervous habit of his to fiddle. Brianna had taken to moving things around on his desk, which had made him have to move things back; this just caused the habit to be a lot worse than it used to be. "I have a gut feeling that there is more to this case than meets the eye, and, well, since the police are still investigating things, I'm going to allow this all to just cool awhile."

"That's not very professional or sound," Adam threatened weakly. "But you do as you wish. We'll just end up dancing in court."

"Yes, we will, and that would be great. I haven't had a good cha-cha in a while. Besides, I love it when judges make my life easier. They just decide things that my boss can't argue with. I love that. Yes, take me to court, Mr. Stillberg," Steven said, sounding calm in his heart and spirit.

Calmness. That was something Breezy's bravery in the face of death had taught him. Stay calm in the face of an adversary. For Breezy, his beloved wife, her tumor was the biggest adversary he had ever faced, and yet their last few weeks together as a family were calm and beautiful, and that was because of her bravery.

"Look, this is going to get ugly," Adam threatened.

"It's already ugly as far as I'm concerned, so . . ." Steven stood. "Do what you've got to do and let me know what you're doing in the meantime. I'll have this file in my office with a Post-it on it that reads 'will deal with later,'" Steven said, making quotation marks in the air around his last few words.

"Yes, well, with that, um, yes, well, my secretary is out to lunch so you'll have to see yourself out."

"Just as I saw myself in," Steven said with a smile. "She takes a lot of breaks," he added, noting the empty front desk in the middle of the lobby. It all spoke to unprofessionalism to him, but then he had a large labyrinth in his office for Brianna, his daughter, to play with when the nanny dropped her off after school— *How unprofessional was that biggo toy.*

Steven could have sworn he heard Adam call him a prick right before he walked out, but he didn't care. Passing the desk of Adam's secretary he noticed the nameplate on her desk. Her name was Victoria. *Old name,* he thought, but then Adam wasn't that young or modern sounding either. He continued to think about the names of the people he was dealing with: Harold, Adam, Phoebe, Lacy, and Marcel.

Glancing at his phone, he realized that he had finally gotten a call back from Marcel DuChamp that had gone to voice mail. He needed to get back to him.

As Steven walked out to meet the elevator on the left, a woman stepped from the elevator on the right. She was pretty, with platinum blond hair and striking blue eyes—the bluest eyes he'd ever seen. They were probably contacts, but still, she was sexy as hell. She had blood red pouty lips and a beauty mark on her face, much like Marilyn Monroe wore—as a matter of fact, she looked a little like Marilyn. Steven found himself giving her more than a sideways glance as she strutted past him into Adam's office. Maybe she worked as a theatre actress because she was a dead ringer for a lookalike actress. He'd seen them before in Vegas.

Right before closing the door, he could have sworn she winked at him. Steven felt a tingle in his groin. Steven hadn't dated much since Breezy's death, but he knew he'd have to start looking soon. It was a strange sensation, but this woman made him sort of think about sex . . .

Funny, huh?

Chapter 28

Lacy was running late, as usual. She was dog tired. She'd dreamed of Marcel all night and got very little sleep. Her allergies were kicking up, too. She'd even had a nosebleed. Never had the air pressure been so heavy inside her house. Despite what the lousy weather girl had promised, the weather up on this hill and in the city was nothing like what it was farther down the coast around Pismo Beach. The Northern California Coast was very different from the Central California Coast and Southern California Coast. The more Lacy thought about it, the more she realized the weather girl was blond and tanned—probably a Southern California Valley Girl. "Doesn't she listen to music . . . phssst, raining in southern California? Yeah, right, like she knows what rain is," The song ran through Lacy's mind before she mentally bashed the weather girl again. *That crazy chick actually predicted sunshine up here, and this close to Thanksgiving, too. My God they so need to fire her. She's so insane,* Lacy thought. It had been raining for weeks—since the start of fall. As a matter of fact, it had been the rainiest year she could remember in a long time. She thought about the funeral, well over a month ago now. It had been raining then too.

Marcel had started a fire. She held him tight while they slept. . . .

Just then her house phone rang. Harriet flipped out. "Shush now," Lacy said, answering it without thinking.

"If I shush you won't hear me," the man said.

Her heart jumped. "Marcel?" she asked, as her mind was filled only with him.

"Why do you keep calling me Marcel? No, this is Harold—"

"Harold?"

"Kitchener. Harold Kitchener."

Lacy's body language showed disappointment. She dropped her folder onto the sofa and folded her free arm around her thickening middle. "I know who you are, Harold."

"I don't want to hold the queenie up but . . ."

"What do you want, Harold?"

"I want to talk about Phoebe—"

"You want to talk about money."

"No, Phoebe, I . . . I think she's haunting me."

"Harold, please!"

"No, seriously. I think she's haunting me and trying to kill me. And—"

Lacy hung up the phone. Grabbing her papers and sunglasses, she hugged Harriet and Oz while ignoring the phone's ringing. "See ya, nasty Pete," she called out.

"You bastard!" Pete called back.

Lacy reached the station, only to find Harold waiting near the door. Seeing her coming, he jumped in front of her on the sidewalk.

"Harold, I'm going to have you arrested!" Lacy said, pushing him aside.

"Damn you're looking hot, Lacy," Harold blurted.

Lacy glared at him for a second. Noticing the knot on his forehead she started to ask about it, but changed her mind before huffing and again charging for the door. Harold blocked her again. She stopped walking.

"Harold, what do you want?"

"Have dinner with me. I need to talk to you. I think we need to talk."

"No."

"Lunch? Come on, Lacy, I need to talk to you. It's serious! I think I was poisoned last night. I ordered take-out from this take-out place me and Phoebe used to go to all the time, and I think they tried to poison me."

"And that concerns me how?"

"It's like she was jealous of me enjoying what we used to enjoy together or something. I mean, she said that one night. She said"—Harold lowered his voice, as if Phoebe would sound anything like a man with a voice deeper than his—"'don't think you're gonna be happy, you prick. You're gonna remember me. . . .'"

"And . . . ?" Lacy sighed.

"And then she poisoned the take-out so I wouldn't enjoy it."

Lacy let out a copious sigh. "Harold, go away."

"We need to talk. I think Phoebe would want it."

"No! And I'm going to call the police if you don't get off my sidewalk!"

"Your sidewalk . . . Damn! Since when did you get so forceful?"

Lacy gave into the moment, and why not? "Since I became queen!" she answered, pushing past him and on into the building. Security greeted her with a smile. She pointed over her shoulder. "That guy there, he can't come near me, okay?"

"Gotcha!" the guard agreed, heading toward Harold, who entered just as she said those words. "Sorry, mister; Ms. Durham said to leave her alone."

"Fine! Fine! I'm not here to see her anyway. I'm here to see my attorney."

Lacy frowned in disbelief.

"Seriously. My attorney's office is upstairs—on the fifth floor," Harold said, no doubt thinking fast on his feet.

There were attorneys on the fifth floor. And Adam Stillberg's office was indeed on the fifth floor, but not the fifth floor of that building. The guard backed off and stood watching as Harold entered the elevator. He waved at Lacy right before the door closed.

"He's lying," Lacy told the guard.

"Well, there are law offices on the fifth floor. So you don't know that."

Lacy wanted to call him a bastard. She quickly realized that she was spending too much time with nasty Pete.

Chapter 29

Adam's face was beet red as he tried to hold on to his control while the woman orally stroked his manhood. It was a great way to get the morning going and the blood pumping. She was a professional at oral sex, of that he was sure. Adam didn't care if he was being used by this woman or the other one, for that matter; all he knew was since this whole insurance matter started he was getting sex. Anyway, anytime he wanted it, one or the other of these women was there to do his bidding. He felt like a king . . . No, better than that, he felt like he'd one-upped Harold Kitchener.

Finally he could hold it in no longer. Grabbing the back of the woman's head he shoved his manhood deep into her mouth and released his emissions. She seemed grateful and pleased to allow him to do so. She was a freak and he loved it. She even swallowed. It was so powerful a thing to watch, to know that a woman had allowed him so much intimacy and closeness without once demanding a thank you or I love you, neither of which came easy for him to say.

"So, how much closer are you to getting Lacy the money?" she asked after a moment of regrouping. She wasn't near done with their sexual encounter. Adam could tell by the way she was rubbing her own body. It was as if she was refreshing herself. She pulled on her own nipples, causing them to raise high off her breasts. Adam was always amazed by the fact that something was so perfect, as her breasts were real. She ran her fingers through her long blond wig, shaking it free as if to clear her head for the next round. She was a dead ringer for Marilyn. She'd even taken on Marilyn's voice and sexy mannerisms. She loved acting.

"I don't want to talk about Lacy. Besides, your little partner said to make sure Harold got the money. I've even made her the beneficiary on his insurance policy—that's the plan, right? He gets the money and then you guys get rid of him, right?"

"What?" the woman said, snapping to attention. Adam sensed he'd said the wrong thing. He regretted it immediately. "Adam, this is my money so it's my plan! It's the only plan you need to listen to! I'm not trying to kill Harold," she said while raking her long nails down his chest. "I was just planning to make his life hell for a while. I was never trying to kill him." She didn't draw blood, but the pain seared through him.

"What about the boat?"

"That was Sonja's plan. It didn't work. So we decided just to drive him crazy until Lacy gets the money. Then we were going to get the money from Lacy."

"How?'

"Technology is a mutha"—she paused long and sexy—"fuck."

She was scaring Adam, yet arousing him at the same time. His manhood began to rise. She noticed. "You want this," she said, turning around to him and spreading her butt cheeks. Adam couldn't speak. He wanted nothing more than to knock at her back door. He'd never been a very sexual man before now. There were many things he'd not experienced. Anal sex was new to him before meeting Harold, Phoebe, and Sonja. He was easily addicted—hooked—on the feeling. The way the women would squeal and moan as if the pain were so bad and yet so good at the same time was beyond a turn-on. Sonja was a freak for anal sex.

"You know I want it," he finally voiced.

She turned back to him. "Then you will do what I say. I want you to tell me everything Sonja says to you. I want you to go along with her as if what she's saying is okay, but then you tell me and I'll let you know it's green, okay, Adam?" she said, kissing his mouth full on. He could taste his semen. He was getting used to that, too. At first it bothered him knowing he was tasting his own emissions and probably those of Harold too. They'd done a couple of threesomes before, but now he was used to it, and he'd do whatever he needed to do to fuck her in the ass.

Turning her around, he bent her over and spread her narrow butt cheeks. Reaching between her legs he felt the cream that had formed around her vulva, and smeared it to the back toward the small opening until she was moist and ready. Parting her anus with his erection again, he was taken to heaven by the sound of her moan, her gasp, and then her high-pitched squeal, as he moved in and out of her tight anal cavity, deeper and deeper until she gave into the rhythm and seemingly began to enjoy the ride.

Chapter 30

Harold hung around upstairs for well over an hour. He'd even decided to have a little breakfast at the deli on that floor. Finally, glancing at his watch, he figured he was safe and got out of the building without any harassment from the guard.

He rushed over to Adam's office. Surely Adam would listen to him. It was his job to listen. It was weird not seeing Victoria at the front desk. He needed to talk to her too. He needed to fix what was broken between them, if he could. He did care about her. She was sweet and pure and nothing like Phoebe.

Glancing at his watch he could see it was lunchtime. "Cold sandwich and a soup," he said, repeating Victoria's order as if he had joined her in line. "She's so predictable," he mumbled under his breath. Passing her desk he reached Adam's office door, but froze hearing the squeals and other sounds that surely didn't belong to Victoria. The sounds were sexual and . . . and familiar. *Who's getting porked in Adam's office? My God, it's the middle of the day,* he thought. "Adam!" he said, speaking Adam's name aloud. Grabbing the knob, he found the door locked. He jerked at it. "Adam, open the door! What's going on in there?" he called out.

"Harold?" Adam called.

"You damn right it's Harold. What's going on in there? I hear . . . I hear something," he said, feeling a little overheated and slightly embarrassed.

Just then the door swung open and Harold got an eyeful of Sonja: long and lovely, with her black hair tossed and her face flushed from the apparently heavy sex. She was barely covering her essentials with Adam's suit jacket.

"You heard something all right, Harold. Now you see something," she said, dropping the jacket, allowing him to get an eyeful of her beyond perfect body. She was slender like Victoria but she was not . . . Victoria. His penis hardened to a substance resembling stone. He wanted to grab at it, control it before it jumped out of his trousers, but he knew he'd have to just let it be and hope that nobody noticed it. His days of fucking Sonja were over. They ended before Phoebe died. They ended the day he walked into his condo and heard sexual sounds coming from his bedroom.

He stepped closer to the door and peeked through the opening in the doorjamb. That's when he saw it: Sonja in a strap-on and Phoebe being butt fucked by her. Phoebe was diggin' it. She was loving it. Begging for more. Harold was beyond jealous. Normally he would have joined the two women, maybe even turned on the camera. Phoebe was a freak for a threesome. He always thought it was just her nature to enjoy group sex with others or others watching; he hadn't even thought she enjoyed sex with others privately . . . especially others like Sonja.

And anal sex at that!

He'd wanted Phoebe to have anal sex with him more than anything. It was the only pleasure from her body he'd not enjoyed and here she was allowing another woman to have the pleasure. He didn't even break them up. He was too busy planning a way to get even with her. Leaving the house, he was fuming mad.

Later that night he again asked Phoebe for anal sex. When she refused he took it. He sodomized her.

Thinking he'd proved his manhood, he was totally caught off guard the next day when Sonja showed up and threatened his life with a knife. Harold realized then that Phoebe was bi-sexual and Sonja was her partner—apparently had been for years, maybe even as far back as high school.

Any more secrets, Phoebe? Harold had asked himself, thinking about the craziest of people who could be the objects of Phoebe's lust—Lacy, maybe, who the hell knew. Maybe even Marcel for that matter.

It took a moment but Adam finally came from his bathroom, zipping up his pants and straightening his tie. His fat face was reddened. Moving in front of Sonja now he took over the doorway. Sonja giggled and moved away from the doorway and back into the office. Harold looked over Adam's shoulder to get a full view of her bending over to gather her clothing that was scattered about.

"Damn," Harold whispered. "Since when . . . ?" Harold asked.

"Since whenever," Adam said, thinking quick on his feet.

"Right, right, but I never knew you two . . . you know. I never knew you were seriously interested in her. I thought you just, you know, were acting," Harold said, winking and blinking.

"There's a lot of stuff you don't know, Harold. Now what do you want? *We* didn't have an appointment and Victoria took the day off." Adam was sounding tense now.

"Sorry, but yeah, anyway, I need to talk to you about Phoebe. I told you that on the phone, and I need to talk to you about the case. I mean, how close are you to finishing this? I'm dying here. I mean, I'm dreaming about Phoebe and it's like—"

"Harold, I'm not a shrink. So see a shrink . . . Go."

"A shrink?"

"Yeah, a brain doctor. I mean, if you can't find anything, or anybody," Adam said, nodding his head toward Victoria's empty desk, "to get your mind off Phoebe, then see a doctor."

Sonja could be heard giggling now as she padded barefoot into the bathroom. Adam looked over his shoulder now, and his jaw line clinched. "Look, Harold, I'll call you," he said, shutting the door in Harold's face. Harold could hear it lock.

"Why isn't anyone listening to me?" he whined. "Phoebe is haunting me. She's trying to kill me and nobody cares. She's blaming me for the boating accident. I know she isssss," he cried out.

"What?" Marcel asked.

Harold spun around to face his former brother-in-law and nemesis, Marcel DuChamp. Marcel had just stepped from the elevator onto Adam's floor. He knew Marcel hated him. Even before he married Phoebe, Marcel hated him. "I know you think I wanted Phoebe dead but I didn't. We weren't happy but there is no crime in that. I know you think I made her make those movies, but I didn't. Phoebe enjoyed the camera. She's dead now and I can't help it."

"What movies, Harold?"

"What? You didn't know?" Harold chuckled. It was unintentional but it slipped. He couldn't believe Marcel didn't know his sister was a porn queen. "She was jealous of Lacy's role as Queen Hynata and so she became queen in her own element. Naked and on her back, where she best served mankind—"

Marcel hit him.

Hard.

Harold hit the floor. Adam's office door flew open. "What the hell?" Adam asked.

"I guess Harold just answered my question about how Phoebe was worth a million dollar insurance policy." Marcel's jaw was tense. His face reddened further at the site of Sonja, half dressed and looking freshly fucked.

Harold, even with his eye covered, noticed that Marcel looked as if he was running out of air. He feared Marcel would explode on everybody. He for one didn't want that. He knew he'd now have a black eye to match the cut on his leg. Phoebe was dead but he was the one being injured here. "I'm outta here," Harold said, scrambling quickly to his feet and rushing to the elevator.

Chapter 31

"So you trying to add a few more days off for your holiday?" Aretha asked. Marcel turned the corner. They were cruising the streets, looking for the suspect of a domestic shooting.

"Please; he deserved that shit."

"You need to stop going off on people. The captain is gonna close this case so tight, you'll think you're fucking with a virgin," Aretha snapped. She was angry. Marcel knew that. She rarely resorted to foul language.

"Aretha." Marcel paused. "My sister did porn. She did . . . porn!"

"Marcel, as a woman—and I am a woman—we all do porn to some degree. We just don't all have the camera rolling or get paid—apparently your sister was talented enough to do both."

"Shit," Marcel sighed.

"Get over it. It was what she enjoyed. If she didn't enjoy it she would have stopped. I mean, it wasn't as if she was forced, was it? Now the important question is not whether she did it, but did she get killed because of it. For one, if Harold was the money guy behind it, chances are he wouldn't want her dead. She was his cash cow."

Marcel grew instantly angry. "Maybe Harold was forcing her. Maybe my sister didn't want any part of that shit! Maybe she knew one day her mother and father would find out and it would kill them."

"Marcel! Get out of the family tree here and listen! Your sister was an adult. Accept that. Now think, if Harold was making money off her 'acting,' why would he kill her? You need to accept that maybe that was not how it went down! You have to start acting like a cop and asking who would truly benefit from her being dead . . . if she's dead!"

"If? Oh now you're finally hearing me."

"I got to thinking. Phoebe is another person who would benefit from this porn queen being dead . . . that is, if she wasn't happy doing it. Maybe she wasn't the one who was supposed to die that day. Who is Harold's beneficiary? Maybe she was miserable and tired of her husband milking her for all he thought she was worth."

"Yeah, she was. She was big-time miserable. I worried about her."

Just then their suspect appeared.

Aretha jumped from the car before it fully stopped. "Hold it right there!" she yelled, but the perp was not going to stop. "You're gonna make me chase you? Oh, man," she yelled, tearing after him.

Marcel too jumped from the car after pulling to a full stop. He hated chasing people through the narrow streets of a neighborhood. He'd been feeling off today and so today was not a good day for it. He had a bad feeling about things and hoped this would go smoothly, but so far it wasn't.

People were starting to peek out of their windows and open their doors. "Go back in!" he yelled, drawing his weapon. He hated having to draw his weapon. Palo Alto had its rough spots but this part, the west end, was crazy.

He and Aretha had been on this case for a while and were now in pursuit of their suspect. Shooting him would make things complicated, including the time spent at the ER hoping he didn't die or, worse, flip the script and act as if he were innocent.

Paperwork on top of paperwork! What a thing to think about when my partner could be in danger, Marcel thought, correcting his thinking as he ran toward the direction he'd seen Aretha chase the thug into.

"Hold your ass right there!" Aretha could be heard screaming from the alleyway. "I got you covered. I'm the police," she yelled. Aretha could be fierce when challenged, and apparently this thug was challenging her big time. Marcel rushed to the alleyway in hopes of backing her up, but he was seconds too late. The suspect fired on him and then attacked Aretha. Marcel was hit in the arm, just grazed, but still.

Aretha's weapon flew from her hands when he kicked her in the face with what looked like a karate move. She fell. He was on her within seconds, pounding on her face.

"Freeze, muthafuck!" Marcel called out before firing a round into the suspect's lower body, trying to miss hitting Aretha entirely while they wrestled on the ground.

Apparently Aretha had taken some pretty tough licks, but as the old watch commercial used to say, she kept on ticking. As a matter of fact, she was about to start a ticking again when Marcel fired.

"Grrrrr," the suspect growled, grabbing at his leg and falling back.

Aretha struggled to her feet. Noticing Marcel bleeding, she reached for her radio. "We need backup," Aretha hollered into it.

Chapter 32

Lacy had begun to think more and more about Harold's panicked call and visit to the station and the insurance money and her conversation with Denise after the funeral. She had tried not to think about the funeral and Phoebe's death too much but the more she tried not to, the more she did.

Every time she looked around her house, she saw the dogs that Phoebe had given her, the comforter that Phoebe had given her as a housewarming gift, the framed picture of the two of them on the high school senior trip. Phoebe had made a point of wanting to take a picture with just her.

Even Pete made her think about Phoebe, with his foul mouth. *He is just like Phoebe.*

Phoebe would be a part of her life . . . *forever.*

Pete the nasty-mouth bird had been in a *fowl* mood—pardon the pun—over the last few days, and she was thinking about taking him to the vet for a tranquilizer of some kind. His tantrums were starting to wear on her nerves.

Even the thought of Marcel brought thoughts of Phoebe, and he'd weighed beyond heavy on her mind and heart. Just then she noticed her phone was blinking. She'd forgotten to take it off silent when she left work. There was a voice mail. It was Denise. "Marcel's been shot. I don't think it's serious but I knew you would want to know. He's at USCF Med—"

Lacy was out the door before finishing the message.

Reaching the hospital, she realized it was probably a mistake when she rushed into the ER only to see several uniformed police officers and Charla. She wasn't in uniform tonight. Lacy froze as their eyes met. It was just as Marcel appeared from the elevator with his arm bandaged up. A black woman was with him. She was laughing as if just having told a joke. Her eye was black, as if she'd gone a couple of rounds, and her nose bandaged. The room seemed to freeze. Lacy cleared her throat and continued on her way to . . . nowhere. Darting around the corner, she quickly dashed into the elevator. Right before it closed she could have sworn she heard Marcel's voice calling her name.

Falling against the back of the small box as it took her to the top floor of the hospital, she sighed heavily. *What were you thinking?* she asked herself. *My God, the weather girl isn't the only one who gets things wrong.*

Chapter 33

Marcel turned off his lights well before he reached the top of the hill. Lacy's house was open and bright. At night it always looked the Emerald City—bright and glassy with the big bay window right there in front. She was easy to see as she walked around inside. He didn't even need the binoculars he had in the glove box.

His arm was stiff but it wasn't the end of the world. The captain had given him the rest of the week off to get better. He didn't need it but he took it. It would be the perfect opportunity to catch up on things. He was planning to meet with Steven Prophet and wanted to have some news, or at least add to whatever Steven had on his end.

They had communicated only a couple of times by phone, and Steven had assured him he was blowing as much smoke as he could to keep this case out of court—at least until they met and had had a chance to really talk.

Marcel watched as Lacy moved around her house. She moved like a dancer—*Wait!* She was dancing. "Oh my God," Marcel sighed while watching her move around the room alone. "This is so wrong, Marcel. This is so very wrong," he said, stepping out of his car as if a magnetic pull was drawing him to the door.

He needed to talk to her though. He needed to say to her all he didn't get the chance to say at the hospital or, worse, in the alley between their parents' homes. Her face had questioned so many things and she deserved answers. She deserved so much more.

Lacy called through the door upon his knock. He could hardly answer her. His voice was stuck in his throat. "I've got a gun," she called.

"So do I," he finally said.

The door swung up and she all but jumped into his arms. He could bear the pain weighted against the pleasure of her body pressed against his.

They moved into her house and on into her bedroom. No words, no questions, no explanations for why so many years had been allowed to pass and so many other people had been allowed into their perfect union of souls. No explanation for why now they seemed to be unable to stay apart.

Her voice was deep and lustful as he entered her hot cavern. She was on fire inside—hotter than the last time. It was as if he'd dived into a warm pie fresh out of his mother's oven—comforting, sweet, and soft. He couldn't thrust deep enough, hard enough, long enough. She gripped his back as if hanging on for life.

Inside Lacy Durham felt like life to him. She felt like the meaning of life for sure.

All too soon, the magic ended. Again they lay together in an awkward space and place in time. "I'm sorry," he finally said.

"I'm not going to cry, Marcel. I'm never going to cry again," she said. Marcel knew she was lying because he wanted to cry too, but he was glad she was at least going to try to be brave for the both of them. Never had he felt so filled with emotion. Uncoupling from her body, he touched and kissed her soft breast that lay bare with nipple raised and hard. He suckled it only to taste sweet nectar. *Had he tasted that the last time?*

"I don't want to do this anymore. I . . . I can't take it," Lacy admitted. "I hope I'm dreaming. I just want to go to sleep now and wake up and pretend this didn't happen."

"Okay," he said, moving out of the bed. He pulled on his pants.

"I'm glad you're not dead, Marcel. I'm glad you didn't get hurt really badly."

"It's my job, you know."

"Yes. I know. But I'm glad you didn't get killed doing it."

Quickly he bent over and kissed her. "Me too, Lace."

Walking from the house the words came from his brain to his lips. "And I love you too," he said.

Chapter 34

Marcel entered the office of Steven Prophet. He was a slender white man with salted black hair. It was obvious the graying was premature as his face was very youthful looking. "Nice to meet you, Detective DuChamp," he said now, reaching out his hand for Marcel to give it a hearty shaking.

"Just call me Marcel. I'm off duty."

"I see. So where do we start?"

"Well, when I called you I wasn't really sure. I just kinda wanted to hear where you were in your investigation. I mean, the delays, why are you delaying paying off the claim?"

Steven looked disappointed and sighed. "Oh, I had hoped you were here to talk about something a bit more substantial than money, like why things don't really make sense in this case."

"Things like?"

"Like why Phoebe Kitchener was insured for a million dollars. She was your sister, right? I mean, you are a cop. Didn't it strike you as funny that your sister was worth a million dollars? Why is Harold Kitchener seeing the woman your sister made beneficiary?"

"Well, first of all, I didn't know she was insured for that much. But, then again, she and Harold had gotten pretty wealthy over the last few years. I had to assume his company was doing well. Secondly, I'm sure you're mistaken when you imply that Harold and Lace are seeing each other. Please explain what you mean by that." Marcel held on to his cool and his words.

Steven stared at him as if looking for something more. But Marcel had nothing more to add to the statement, so Steven continued to speak. "Didn't you wonder why she left all that money to a friend and not her spouse? Wouldn't it make you think something was strange? And then to see them . . . or at least it looked like her going into his apartment last night around ten P.M. She had red hair and—"

"Well, now, that would have made me wonder, I'd have to say. Sure, that would seem very plausible. But seeing as how I've had my eye on Lacy Durham fairly closely, I'd have to argue that she's not seeing Harold Kitchener on anything other than a purely accidental basis. I mean, he did show up at her job the other day, but that's it. As far as why my sister didn't leave him the money, if he's seeing someone in a romantic way, then that should tell you something about his character, if you get my meaning. . . ." Marcel shook his head in disgust at that thought of Harold.

"So he's a jerk? I had a feeling he was a jerk but wasn't sure. I also wasn't sure that was Lacy Durham. She won't return my calls so—"

"Oh yeah, big-time jerk, and no, that wasn't Lacy Durham you saw last night. She was home . . . all night."

"Really. So you've been following Ms. Durham?"

"Yes and no . . ." Marcel said, again holding on to his words.

Steven raised an eyebrow but kept talking. "Well, Mr. Kitchener called me within days of your sister's death. I mean, before the funeral he called about the money."

"He did? Really?"

"And he knew the amount that she was insured for, too, but he sure as heck didn't know he wasn't the beneficiary."

"That's weird. I mean, almost as weird as Phoebe leaving the money to Lacy Durham."

"So you know Ms. Durham—personally?"

Marcel's face must have shown the truth about how well he knew Lacy Durham, as Steven just smiled.

"Let's just say we're all old friends. I mean, Harold, Lacy, me, and Phoebe, we all went to school together."

"Ahh."

"But Lacy and Phoebe weren't that close. I mean they were close, but not that close."

"So why do you think she left her the money?"

"Wish I knew, and I believe Lacy when she says that she wishes she knew too."

"So you've spoken to her?"

Again Marcel's face gave him away. Steven smiled again. He was a comfortable man and Marcel instantly felt that they had a level of relating without having to spell it out. He'd all but said he was keeping an eye on Lacy from close up and at a distance. Steven didn't appear to be a naïve man, so he didn't feel the need to tell his business or embarrass Lacy that way by kissing and telling. "Yeah, I talked to her the night of the funeral. That's when I found out myself that she was a beneficiary. I found out from another of our former classmates. Trust me, Lacy didn't know before that day either."

"Crazy," Steven said, rubbing his chin. Both men were still standing as they had jumped right into this conversation after shaking hands. It was like a boxing round. At this point now, however, Marcel looked around Steven's simple office. He noticed the large labyrinth and pictures of the obviously mixed-race little girl hanging in large black-and-whites along the wall.

One of the large pictures stood out in particular; it was of the little girl in a playful-looking embrace of a fair-skinned black woman with a mop of curls on her head. They looked loving and happy. "Your family?" Marcel asked, pointing at the picture.

"My wife. She died last year."

Marcel was hit with instant sadness for the man. "Oh God, I'm sorry."

"Me too. I loved her very much. She and that little girl made up my world."

"How is your daughter doing?"

"She's okay. She'll be here in a bit. I'll need to cut this short. It's pizza night for us."

"I got you on that." Marcel chuckled, wondering what Charla had planned for dinner. He instantly thought about Lacy, wondering what she may have planned . . . *for the rest of her life.* The thought made him shake his head to clear it. He'd been having those kinds of thoughts about Lacy for a couple of weeks now. Watching her had become almost like coming home at night. It was comfortable and invasive. He all but stalked her, watching her through the large bay windows, cooking and talking to that bird. Petting her dogs and then flopping on the sofa where they had slept together, and going to sleep. She'd yet to go into her bed. He wondered why, but in his deepest of hearts he too had been troubled in the sleep department.

Right after the morning spent with Lacy, he had gone home. Charla was waiting as always. She'd gotten off work and was home watching television before turning in. She was planning to pull a graveyard shift. She never told him about her shift changes before accepting them. It was as if she always took for granted that he was cool with her never being there for him at night. He wasn't.

She didn't even seem to notice that he didn't kiss her or greet her the way he used to. They were falling apart. Sure, he loved her, but not like he used to. He had to realize that if he did, sleeping with Lacy may not have happened so easily. *That's a lie, Marcel. You've wanted to see Lacy again for long time. Get your balls out of your pocket and admit it. You've always loved her, wanted her. You're dumb and full of stupid pride and it has cost way too many years of your miserable life.*

Realizing that Steven was speaking, Marcel mentally rejoined the conversation. "I'm sorry, what?"

"No. I'm sorry. I said I'm glad your sister didn't have any children, but that may have not been a nice thing to say and I'm sorry."

"No. It's okay. She lost a baby last year. She fell. They sued and won. I mean, they won a lot of money, but you ask me"—Marcel shook his head again to clear his thoughts—"money will never replace a life. Even her life seemed so different after that. I didn't see my sister regularly and it was my mom who told me about the baby. But when I did see her after that, she just wasn't the same."

"Oh, I totally get you."

"But, then again, had she had the baby, who knows where that child would be now."

"God, I'm so with you on that," Steven said, holding out his hand to be slapped. Marcel chuckled slightly at what he commonly felt to be a "black" thing. Maybe being married to a black woman had changed him a little bit. Marcel often wondered about a life with Lacy—seeing as how she was mixed. He thought about Lacy's father. He was always slapping five and talking jive. He was a very smart man, but he enjoyed playing around and joking. He liked making light of what people felt would offend. Marcel enjoyed talking to him.

"Well, I won't keep you, Steven. I came because I think my sister was murdered. I don't think that was an accident. I think her husband killed her."

"My gosh. What a leap! I mean, I smelled some fraud going on for sure. I mean that Barry Nugent, well, let's just say his boat story wasn't floating with me—pardon the pun. But murder? What makes you reach there?"

"Well—"

Just then the door burst open and a charmingly beautiful little girl burst in. "Daddy!" she squealed as if she'd not seen him in weeks instead of the hours it had probably been. He scooped her up in his arms.

"Hey, precious. Say hello to the policeman," Steven said, pointing at Marcel.

The little girl turned and waved shyly. "Is my daddy in trouble? Did he get another ticket?"

Marcel and Steven burst into laughter. "Leave it to a child to put your life on blast," Steven said.

"I wouldn't know. I don't have any."

"Well I'd say you're fortunate, but only in that way." Steven laughed and then kissed his daughter's cheek while walking toward the door. Marcel took the hint and headed that way too. "Detective, please, let's not leave it at speculation. I'm willing to do my part to delay this as long as I can if it will help you get to the truth," Steven said, showing Marcel out.

"Thank you."

Chapter 35

"Have you even seen Phoebe?" Sonja asked Adam.

"No."

"You're fuckin' lying. . . ." Sonja answered, fondling his bottles of pills that sat on his desk: indigestion tablets, headache medicines, Pepcid for his ulcer.

"Seriously, I haven't seen her. But it's okay, in a way it's good she's not coming around. I've been needing to talk to you . . . alone."

"About what, big boy?" Sonja said vampishly. She moved quickly around the desk and reached for his crotch.

He allowed her the wandering hands routine for just a moment. She reached into his trousers and that's when he stopped her. "It's too early in the day and, well, this is actually business."

"Okay. Shoot!"

"Okay," Adam said, gulping at air. "Here's the deal: I say we cut everybody out and you and me take the money and run."

"Why? Why would I do that to Phoebe?"

Adam reached in his drawer and pulled out some forms. "Read this."

"What is it?"

"Phoebe's new will."

Sonja took it from him. As she read, her eyes widened. "She wants me to backdate it and act like she wrote it before she died."

"What the fuck, man! You said you hadn't seen her!" Sonja screamed. "Are you kidding me? She's got some balls trying to cut me out this way! And you! You!" Sonja's voice was nearly at a screech now. "You tell me how she was gonna pull this off! You tell me what she's planning!"

Adam's eyebrow rose slightly. "Who knows what she's planning."

"I don't believe any of this, Adam," Sonja said, tossing the papers on the desk. "And why would you even draw this up for her unless you were gonna get something out of it? I can't even imagine you doing this without a promise."

Adam just smiled. "I'm not one to kiss and tell. . . ."

"You bastard!" Sonja yelped, shoving his cup of coffee over until it spilled into his lap. It had cooled, but still he yelped and jumped up from his seat because of the mess. "You were going to let Phoebe screw all of us out of a million dollars, and more if you count Harold's properties and stuff! You tell me how you were going to get Harold to agree to sign all his shit over to Phoebe *after* she's dead. Oh, you were just gonna forge his signature as if he wasn't gonna notice."

"She was talking crazy. None of her crazy plan was going to work. I mean, why do you think I'm telling you about it, baby?" Adam said, trying to regain her trust.

Sonja began to pace the room. "You are a liar," she finally decided. "You were going to let her cut me out—"

"Sweetheart, even if I did go along with this crazy thing," Adam said, easing over to Sonja's side where she stood pouting, "you'd have me. Don't think I couldn't work these papers where you and me could get enough to go away with. I mean, who cares about Harold, right? Who cares if Phoebe is with someone else—"

"She's with someone else!" Sonja screamed.

Just then Victoria entered the office without knocking. "Adam! Oh, I didn't know you had company," she said, eyeing Sonja over from head to toe.

"Well he does have company! Get out," Sonja insulted.

"Adam!" Victoria whined.

"Sonja, stop!"

Sonja stormed toward the door, brushing briskly past Victoria. "I'll be back, Adam! I think this is the perfect moment to leave. I'll let you visit with your loving sister . . . You know, the one you love so much."

"Sonja, where are you going?" Adam asked.

"To raise hell," she spat before slamming the door.

Chapter 36

Sonja burst into Harold's office. His secretary raced behind her only to have Harold dismiss her. "To what do I owe this honor?" he said to Sonja, who clearly appeared out of breath.

"I've got something to tell you and you'd better listen to me."

"Okay," he said, moving to his side of the desk. It wasn't as if he trusted Sonja all that much.

"Adam is trying to fuck you over for the money."

"He can't. I'm gonna win the case . . . Slam dunk."

"Slam dunk in your face, asshole. I'm telling you and I know—Adam has an ace in his pants and he's gonna use it."

"And what is that?" Harold asked smugly.

"Phoebe."

"Phoebe is dead. Whatever she did before she died, died with her. Remember, that's what you told me while trying to comfort me," Harold said coolly.

"Harold, did you recently have a dream where Phoebe came to your bed and cut you on the leg?"

Realizing that Sonja knew something that she shouldn't know, he gulped air and started really listening to her.

"Did you have a dream where she fucked you like crazy?" Sonja went on.

"Yeah."

"Yeah, like I said . . ."

"You're telling me Phoebe is alive!"

"Yeah, and so are you . . . unfortunately."

"What?"

"You haven't figured it out, asshole. You were supposed to die in that boating accident."

"Me? Why?"

"Because little Miss Purity was tired of the porn game. She wanted out and you weren't giving it to her."

"Phoebe loved making porn. She was a natural at it. She was—*is*—a freak."

Sonja moved over to Harold's side of the desk. Suddenly she grabbed a handful of his hair. "We all are, I guess. But there comes a time when other things start to become more important."

Harold grunted at the pain. "Other things?"

"Yeah, like love, babies, and shit like that there."

"You're telling me that Phoebe wanted out to have a baby?" Harold asked, pulling free from her grip.

"Crazy, huh? You know all those accidentally-on-purpose accidents you and Adam planned?"

"Don't know what you mean," Harold lied. He was shocked at what Adam had told Sonja. Could it be she was right about him and that he was truly a traitor? That Phoebe and Sonja had him pussy whipped? *That's what I get for hiring a fat fuck loser who never got laid much,* Harold thought quickly about Adam.

"Sure, you do. The store, the car accident, the fall . . . Remember she lost that baby," Sonja said, rubbing Harold's chest seductively while moving behind him to speak in his ear.

"Okay, fine but . . ." Harold turned to her only to meet her lips.

After the kiss she gazed into his eyes. "I heard something go boing the minute she found out that baby was gone. She snapped, Harold. She started talking about school days and old friends and family and going home. That's what she wanted, Harold. She hated you after that and swore she'd get even with you."

"So she was gonna kill me?"

"Have you checked your insurance policies lately? You're insured up the wazoo with her as a beneficiary. She named Lacy because, well, for one she didn't plan on dying and for another, personally, I think she's got a little crush on her." Sonja's last words rang to the tune of jealousy. Harold recognized it.

"So that bitch was gonna kill me?"

"Yep."

"Where is she now?"

"Who the hell knows? We got into it and she took off."

"Ahh, a little lovers' quarrel?"

Sonja smiled wickedly. "Oooh but the makeup sex is sooo good."

"Bitch."

"Hey, don't knock me till you try me," Sonja smarted off.

"Yeah, right. So why you fuckin' Adam."

"Please, why does anybody fuck Adam?"

They both burst into laughter.

"So what do I need to do?"

"We need to do?"

"Leave it to me. We just need to get Lacy out of the picture and the rest will fall into place."

"Okay. Not sure what you've got in that pretty little head of yours. But . . ." Harold walked over to his door. He peeked out into the empty lobby. He smiled at Rosa, his secretary, and then locked the door. "But I do know what I have in this pretty little head of mine," he said, unbuckling his belt. Sonja smiled.

Harold always enjoyed the fact that he had women like Phoebe and Sonja in his life. It was a man's fantasy for sure. They would do anything sexually and it meant nothing.

Obviously! Here he was thinking Phoebe enjoyed her work and then he finds out that she was plotting to kill him. "Bitch," he said aloud. Sonja seethed as if the word itself turned her on. He thrust harder into her cavern, which he was taking from the back. He wanted more. He wanted what he craved but he'd wait until the time was right. Right now he just needed to calm his nerves the easiest and best way he knew how—and seal this partnership with a *kiss*. A couple of quick twists of her hips had his semen flowing like water through her cistern.

"How come you never get pregnant, Sonja?" he asked her later. "As much as you fuck—"

"Horse riding accident," she said flatly, while running her fingers through her hair.

"You mean horseback riding," Harold corrected.

Sonja smiled wickedly. "I know exactly what I meant."

Chapter 37

Victoria squirmed in her bed. She'd not had Harold in what felt like forever, although it hadn't been nearly that long. She was tense. Sonja's visit to her brother's office today had upset her very much. She was on fire between her legs. It was shameful how much she enjoyed sex with Harold.

She knew Harold was not a "good boy" and she probably should not have had anything to do with him, but sex was a huge draw and she, being of little experience, was caught up now, like a fly in a spider's web.

He had her at go. Every time he came to the office he would wink at her. Once he even brought her a rose. She about fainted.

Still married to Phoebe, Harold Kitchener had started coming to Adam's office just about a year ago. They seemed to have a lot of business to take care of. She'd tried to get it out of Adam if maybe he was getting divorced or something, but Adam's lips were sealed. But then she noticed Harold's wife, Phoebe, coming into the office to see Adam . . . alone.

She wasn't planning to spy, but she couldn't help but hear them in the office. Victoria wasn't a virgin; she knew what they were doing in there and she was shocked. She was appalled and then, as it went on and on, she became aroused. She felt dirty hearing her brother moan and groan and go on like a wounded animal with that woman Phoebe.

But, then again, Phoebe DuChamp was beautiful. She remembered in school all the boys talked about her. Victoria was a freshman when she and Harold were seniors so that gave her the vantage point to hear all and say nothing, at least nothing anybody cared about.

Phoebe was promiscuous, all the girls who hung with her were—well, except that girl Lacy Durham, and from what she heard Lacy was the only one to make anything of herself. Sure, that girl Sonja went on to become a big model overseas but, still, dressing up just to show off your clothes wasn't really a career—*if you ask me,* Victoria thought, sliding into her shoes.

She was nearly dripping wet at the memory of Phoebe and her brother sexing like animals in his office that day. After that she felt it was her duty to tell Harold what she'd heard.

They met for lunch at the Hilton Hotel restaurant. She felt bad but he had to know. He seemed so broken up about it that she held his hands tight while he went on to tell her how lonely of a marriage he had. She knew she was being foolish, but she wanted to believe she was helping him.

She went to the hotel room with him that afternoon. Maybe she felt making him wear a condom was enough to make it okay, but what he did to her with his mouth and fingers—*oh my gosh,* she thought, sighing and sliding into her jacket.

She'd never had a man put his tongue between her lower lips before—licking, kissing, and sucking on her clit like that. She'd never had a man feast between her legs as if she were a fancy meal. He then entered her full thrust, pulling her legs over his shoulders. Victoria bit her bottom lip with the memory of their first time. She bit her lip to keep from letting out a cry of passion as she started up her car and headed to Harold's condo.

He'd given her the key long before Phoebe died. She'd never used it, though. It was almost as if he wanted her to. It was as if he wanted them to get caught in his condo making love. *There's no way I would do something like that.* But the night after Phoebe died, she made love in that house, in that bed, and in every room of that condo. *He needed it. He was a broken man. He needed to feel better,* Victoria reasoned.

Reaching the condo, she saw he wasn't home. She went in and on up to the bedroom. Surely he'd be home soon. He liked it when she was waiting naked in the bed. While she lay there, she noticed the bottle of wine. He always had a little before bedtime. She poured herself a full glass of it—more than a little. But tonight she needed it. She was horny and planning to sex him the way she'd seen Phoebe and Sonja do it in those movies. Tonight she was going to make him forget about Phoebe, the money, and all else. Tonight she was going to make him ask her to marry him.

Chapter 38

Steven patted his camera, which sat in the seat next to him. Surprisingly enough he was a little nervous. He wasn't sure what he was going to see, but if he saw what he thought he might, he'd have enough evidence to raise the suspicion levels a little higher on this insurance case. There were a lot of little things that just didn't seem right. *Sure, if ill-fitted pieces to this puzzle were just being set aside for the obvious, the obvious wouldn't be the most important thing,* he thought, remembering one of his college professors who was big on the old adage of trusting none of what you hear and only half of what you see.

Marcel DuChamp was obviously siding with Lacy Durham on this case. *I kinda am too, but I want to make sure there is no hanky-panky going on. I mean, Harold is seeing a woman who could just as easily be Lacy Durham. If they are playin' bait and switch here, this whole thing could just explode with intrigue. Wouldn't that be wild, to find out Lacy and Harold were in cahoots?*

Just then he saw the woman getting out of a cab. From the lights inside the cab he could see for just a moment before she closed the door that she was redheaded. The curls hung loose around her shoulders. He was fairly sure he'd seen her at Harold's place before. Was she the same woman? He had to be sure. Was she the same one? Who could know? He'd made a point of trying his best to get a visual of all the players in this case, and despite the fact that he'd not met her face to face, from a distance this looked like none other than Lacy Durham.

The woman didn't look around. It was as if she was confident that she had not been followed nor was she being watched in his suburban neighborhood. She walked as if she belonged here. But then again, Steven noticed, as with many suburban neighborhoods, at ten P.M. most of the homes on the street had their lights out.

"Damn! I need to see her face!" Steven said, hustling up his equipment and climbing out of his car. He had to get a closer look and pictures. He waited before creeping up to the door of the condo, until the woman, using a key, went in. He wasn't a spy or a P.I., although both career choices would have been fine with him. He tried to see in the windows but couldn't. The shrubs were too high and there was no way he was climbing up on anything. He'd watched too many Disney movies with Brianna to trust that he wouldn't fall loudly and be caught. It wouldn't be funny if it happened to him this night. Looking around, he dashed across the street to see if any lights would come on, and sure enough the upstairs eventually showed a dim light, such as one given off by a flashlight or a small luminary—maybe even a candle. He took a couple of pictures that would probably be useless, before getting back in his car.

He watched for what was about an hour before the front door opened and the woman stepped from the house. She walked up the street, only to have the cab come around the corner as if arranged. She climbed in and left. He started up his car to follow.

Chapter 39

Adam wasn't really all that hungry. He'd made a dinner date and he'd planned to eat out then. As far as he was concerned, it was for dinner that he'd agreed to meet Harold at a local pub. He didn't want to talk to Harold, but if he kept refusing, *soon this idiot is gonna figure out something,* Adam thought, turning up his tumbler and draining his glass.

Besides, he needed to talk to Harold before Steven Prophet did. Steven really didn't need to hear Harold ranting on and on about being haunted. Steven Prophet was becoming a problem. For that matter, Sonja was too. She had lost her damn mind. He needed to give her a few days to cool off after her tirade in his office. She was going to blow this whole thing going off the deep end like that.

It was so ironic that Harold ended up even being a part of this whole thing. It was just by accident that he was even still alive. But, in the end, it was going to work out. He would get the money and he would marry Victoria, which would mean she would get the money, and then that would mean he would get the money, and that would mean Sonja would get the money. Adam's thoughts stopped abruptly at Sonja. There was no way in hell she would be patient enough to wait for all that to happen. Sonja was a woman with her own agenda. And at any given moment, Adam hadn't a clue what that agenda was. It didn't matter. He was hot for her and wanted her body all the time. Sure, he was getting his fill of pussy these days from both women, but Sonja was the woman of his dreams. Adam knew that Sonja was the woman of Harold's dreams as well, but he never stood a chance with her, not with Phoebe around. Phoebe was a whole lot easier to get than Sonja. Adam had found that out the easy way.

Wouldn't that be an eye opener though? Adam's thoughts continued. *To realize that in the end you aren't the only one who can get both girls.* In school, Adam always envied Harold. Being a year younger, he knew Harold didn't know he existed; none of the in crowd did. That elite group of cool kids never paid him half a mind. He was chubby and awkward, and they thought they were gods and goddesses. But Phoebe was a goddess, at least in Adam's opinion. She was the prettiest girl he'd ever met. He would all but drool watching her play tennis on the courts. She never even noticed him, not even when he handed her towels when she came from the water during her swim meets. Yeah, she was champion swimmer. That was one reason it was easy for him to come up with this plan. He knew Harold was planning for her to have another "accident." He found out really quickly that she was a cash cow of clumsiness.

And suing that construction company for shoddy work when Phoebe lost that baby was the best move ever. Harold was able to even open his own construction company with the money from that. Ironically he hired the very same guys who built this house to work for him.

Ooooh was Pheebs pissed. Harold is such a prick. Adam thought, chuckling under his breath. *And then there is Sonja. . . .*

Just then, before Adam could complete his fantasy, Harold burst into the pub. "Adam! Somebody just tried to run me down!"

"What?"

"Outside. That's why I'm late. I mean truly, I actually . . ." Harold looked down at his dirty clothes. "I actually had to dive out of the way!"

"Did you get a look at the driver?"

"No. But I know who it was. It was Phoebe. I'm not dreaming. She's back from the dead and trying to kill my ass for all the horrible things I did to her. She's trying to kill me for making her do those porn movies and for basically setting her up to have those accidents." Harold was confessing all his sins right out in the open. "No wonder she didn't leave her money to me. I'm a horrible person, Adam," Harold cried, grabbing Adam's lapels. "And now I'm going to be haunted the rest of my life until I die like I should have done on that boat!"

Adam stared at him. He was caught speechless by Harold's outburst. For a second he almost wanted to confess to him all he knew to be true. But he couldn't. He couldn't tell Harold anything. He hated Harold and suddenly pitied him at the same time. "Harold," Adam began. "You should have called the police."

"No. That would only piss her off more. I deserve all she's doing. I need to just . . ." He caught himself.

"Harold, get a hold of yourself. Here, have a drink," Adam said, fanning over the waitress.

Harold was clearly and visibly shaken. "Something's going on, Adam." He pulled up his pant leg, exposing his bandage. "Look. She cut me. She came into my place and cut me."

"That's crazy, Harold. You must be sleepwalking again. Victoria told me you sleepwalk."

"Victoria told you that? She talked to you about *us?*" Harold was instantly sidetracked.

"Of course. My sister is, you know . . . Suffice it to say, you're a bit worldly for her," Adam said, still not giving into Harold's excitement over the near-death experience he'd just had.

"Well, um . . . Yeah, I guess sometimes I do walk in my sleep, but only lately. Lately it's been real bad. I mean, Victoria would only know since Phoebe died. I mean, we didn't sleep together until Phoebe died."

"Harold, you don't have to defend yourself to me," Adam said, snickering wickedly. "You're acting like we don't know each other . . . well," Adam added, hoping to make Harold remember the threesomes they had with Phoebe while filming.

Phoebe had turned out to be such an insecure woman, even more so after she lost that baby. Adam was continually amazed that she'd even allowed herself to get knocked up. The thought that he could possibly be the father of the baby made Adam smile. He'd not ever had anyone accuse him of impregnating them before Phoebe. It was kind of exciting.

Harold didn't see it that way. Before the news of her pregnancy could get too far, Phoebe had an accident and the baby was gone.

"Hey, dude, check out that shiner. I thought it'd be gone by now."

"Oh yeah, I need to sue my brother-in-law, by the way."

"For what?"

"Harassment or something."

"Nah, I think the quieter you are right now the better it will be for all of us. The less attention you draw to yourself, the better."

"Yeah, maybe you're right. I'm just . . . I don't know, Adam. I'm just tired, and wish this whole thing was over."

"Well." Adam patted his shoulder. "That's what I'm here for, to make it all go away. Go on home. I'll talk to Victoria tomorrow. I'm sure she's past ready to take you back."

Chapter 40

Marcel pulled up to the Chinese take-out restaurant. Charla unbuckled her seat belt. They'd had a pleasant day off together—and, to be truthful, he wasn't sure which was the rarer of events: the pleasantness or the day off, as lately Charla hadn't been the most loving woman to be with. Even this day, she'd not even attempted to insinuate that they would have sex. Sure, Marcel wanted sex. He wanted sex with Charla. He figured sex with her would fix it. He didn't hate Charla. He cared about her. He cared a lot. He wanted to fix what he'd broken. Sure, Charla didn't know he'd broken anything, but he did.

She wasn't stupid. She'd noticed Lacy showing up at the hospital. She even asked him about it, in a sideways kind of way. Marcel came up with some lame excuse of her possibly being there to entertain children in the children's ward.

"She is a cartoon shero, for crying out loud," he said.

Charla nodded as if she hadn't thought about it. "Yeah, a shero that got her ass kicked not too long ago."

"What?"

"We had a call up on that hill. I guess the queen had tried to break up with her boyfriend and he wasn't having it. She ended up pulling a gun on him, but not before he'd tried to knock her block off."

"Really?"

"Yeah, really. I have to admit, I was impressed that she wasn't crying and all that other girlie stuff. Chick had a gun. I can totally get with that," Charla said, sounding sincere.

Leaning over, he caught her arm. She glanced at him and smiled. "I . . ." Marcel began. He wanted to say something that was pretty close to "I love you" but he couldn't. To make it worse, the only woman who had ever generated those words, Lacy Durham, came bounding out of the restaurant right at that moment. She had a huge bag of food. Surely more than one person could eat. He looked around to find her car. He expected to see a man waiting, a date, but he only saw the dogs jumping around in the seat, excited to see her returning with what they probably thought were treats. She was glowing and beautiful. Her hair was loose and bouncy with rich red curls. His eyes followed her until they met Charla's awaiting gaze.

"You what?" she asked.

"I want, um . . . a number three. Yeah, just order me a number three," he said. Her face dropped and she climbed out of the car. It was obvious she was irritated as she slammed the door. Walking toward the entrance, she pulled out her cell phone. His stomach tightened. He could only guess who was on the other end—another of her male-bashing friends.

There would be no romantic dinner tonight. Pulling out his cell phone, he dialed Lacy's number. *Why the hell not,* he thought. *What worse could I do? Besides, I need to know how she's holding up,* he internalized. The phone rang but he only saw her driving off as if on fire. Lacy was no doubt on a mission. He envisioned her buying dinner for her and a boyfriend to share.

Just then Aretha called him. "Hey, get down here. Got a body you just gotta see!"

***

Officers were at the scene roping off the perimeter when Marcel arrived. Marcel walked in the front door of Harold's nicely furnished condo and on up the stairs to the living room. One of the officers on the scene pointed to the bedroom. There in the bed lay the corpse of a naked dark-haired woman, face down. She was slender and had what looked like a fresh tattoo on her rear end. Turning, he heard Aretha coming in the front door. He went out to greet her.

"Got a name?"

"You sure took your sweet time getting here."

"I came as fast as I could, considering I'm off today. Got a name?"

"You smell like Bubba's Chinese Palace," she observed while getting totally off track. "You out on a date?"

"Who's dead in there, Aretha?"

"Was it a date with the queenie or the meanie?"

"Aretha!"

"Okay, okay! Her name is Victoria Stillberg. Ring any bells?"

"Victoria?"

About that time, Harold burst through the officers blocking the door. "What the hell is going on here?"

Chapter 41

"Got you!" Steven said, snapping the picture as soon as the door opened. It was right before she pushed him. Steven was caught off guard and stumbled back, dropping the camera in the flower pot that sat along the railing. He'd followed the cab all the way out to Pacifica. The house was large and nestled in the middle of a quiet, unsuspecting block.

The dark-haired woman stepped quickly toward it, but Steven tried to move faster, grabbing the camera. The woman kicked him—more than once. She had strong legs and kicked with the power far and above what he expected from a woman of her thin frame. She probably could have taken him, even without the baseball bat.

Crack. . . .

Down the eight concrete steps he went. Hitting his head on the way down, he heard the bone crack, but couldn't feel any pain so he wasn't sure what she'd broken on him. That was the worst kind of injury. He knew that from his days as a football player in school. Sometimes he wouldn't know he'd broken something until after the game, after running that touchdown. But he wasn't gonna make a score tonight. Tonight he was going to be murdered if he wasn't careful, and in the end it was going to look like something it was not—of that he was certain. It was going to take a good cop to put the dots together on this one if he was killed tonight.

Why was he there? Who was he following? Who was the mysterious redheaded woman? Hell, he had the same questions.

As she stepped over him, ripping the camera from his hands, he could hear the film being taken out and her throwing the camera aside. He knew he hurt badly but he was probably going to die before anyone would find him, or help him. He couldn't feel his legs, or his arms; he couldn't feel anything.

Just then, before closing his eyes, he had what he thought was a fantasy. The woman from Adam's office, the one who looked like Marilyn Monroe, stared into his eyes. This night, she had dark hair and deep, dark eyes that were widened with what looked like fear. She argued with the other woman for a moment. He heard the screech of tires and then Marilyn's soft voice. "I'm sorry. I'll call for help. Oh my God . . . this is so out of hand. I'm sorry. I . . ."

Steven lost consciousness.

Chapter 42

Dave opened the door to find her standing there. She'd been crying out loudly, calling his name, which woke him and drove him quickly to his door.

"I didn't do it, Dave. I swear it. I got to Harold's, I was going to tell him the truth, and Victoria was there. She was dead. Oh God." She spoke quickly. Her hands were shaking. Dave pulled her inside and shut the door.

"Slow down, sweetheart. Slow it down."

"Victoria was dead already. I knew Sonja had been there. She had to have done it. He had this." She held out the rain-drenched camera. Again the rains had come in on top of the hill. Dave took the camera from her. "I freaked out. I freaked out! Sonja hit him with the bat. The bat has my prints on it. Everything at that house has my prints on it. I went there to get some things. I knew after they found Victoria they would come after me—I knew they would figure it out. My prints are all over Harold's place too. Eventually they would figure it out and they would come after me. So I was trying to get outta there. Sonja and I were going to take the money and go to France. Sonja is out of control, so I was just going to ask Adam to give me the money to go now. Things are out of control. Oh God," Phoebe cried.

Dave said, "Raven," as he now called her. "You're safe now. You're safe."

"I think he's dead, and if he's not dead he'll recognize me," she cried.

"Did he get a good look? I mean, were you in disguise?"

"No. I looked just like this," Raven said, pointing at herself, wet and without makeup.

"Well." Dave sighed. "You'll never look like this again," he assured her. "We have to work fast but you have to tell me again, why did you do this? Why did you do all of this?"

They shared a quiet moment as Raven seemed to regroup. "I did it because I wanted a new life. I hated Harold and what he was turning me into. I hated Adam Stillberg for wanting me as if I was a menu choice at McDonald's. I hated Sonja . . . I *hate* Sonja for trying to tell me who I can love and who I can't, and I love Lacy Durham. I love her." Raven began to cry. "I just wanted to spend the rest of my life with her up here on this hill. It was stupid and I didn't know how it was going to happen, but I was going to make it happen. Maybe I was going to change my looks in France and eventually come back. I would pretend to be someone sweet and nice and I was going to make her be my friend. Hell, she was going to be rich; maybe she would hire me as a maid. I don't know." Raven chuckled. "Imagine that: me, Phoebe DuChamp, the most popular girl in school, begging for the friendship of the biggest nerd in the world, Lacy Durham." Raven smiled. "But nobody knew her like I did. I don't think she even knows herself like I do. She lives my life. She's always lived my life. She's like the bumblebee, ya know? A bumblebee is not even supposed to fly, but nobody told it that it couldn't, so it does. That's Lacy."

"And what about me?" Dave asked cautiously. He knew he was getting in over his head—way over his head—but up to this point he could relate to all she'd said. He loved Lacy too. He loved her life, and before meeting her he'd hated his own, but watching Lacy "fly" against all odds had given him so much hope. She'd turned from an ugly duckling to a swan . . . Hell, to Queen of the Amazon.

"And then I met you, and I didn't just fall on those rocks. I fell in love with you. I didn't intend to; it just happened. You saved my life that day on the rocks. Now save me again, Dave."

Dave picked up his phone. He was going to need to call in a favor.

Chapter 43

"Gentlemen, let me assure you that this was no accidental overdose. This woman was murdered," Sam said calmly. It wasn't as if he was being questioned but, still, hearing him say it brought reassured nods all around. "She had enough Flunitrazepam in her system to nearly paralyze her; nonetheless, her killer didn't stop there, but continued to administer a deadly mixture of aluminum hydroxide."

Aretha, Marcel, Lawrence, and Jim all gave Victoria Stillberg a closer look. "These burns here around the mouth and throat were caused by a mixture of aluminum hydroxide and some other chemical, probably acid in a simple form. My guess is it was foreign, as I can't seem to find it in our list of chemicals commonly found here in this country. My guess is it was probably a painful death, too, yet there were no signs that she vexed or fought death. That was probably due to the Flunitrazepam in her system."

"Flunitrazepam? That's Rohypnol, right?" Lawrence asked.

"So, with the rophy in her system, she could have believed this was all just part of a bad trip?" Jim added.

Sam nodded. "Possibly. Now, this aluminum hydroxide mix was found just recently in another victim— the one you two brought in—no Flunitrazepam, but nonetheless the acid-like mixture. That is why I called you all here."

"Don't tell me this is some new kind of freaky drug party," Aretha blurted.

"Heavens no. The other victim convulsed and clearly showed signs of a struggle to stay alive. He had no rophy in his system and felt the full effect. Oh, and I put his time of death to have occurred during daylight hours. Not really a party scene if you get me," Sam explained.

"You found another body that looked like this one?" Marcel asked.

Sam nodded vigorously. "Yes," he said, moving to another drawer and rolling out the corpse of Boyd Jameson.

"Didn't know what to make of it when we found him," Jim said. "ID in place and everything. Had no clue who would have killed him or how."

Marcel flinched. "Yikes. Who is he?"

"Jameson was a bio tech for one of the major companies out in Emeryville. Made a little side money selling illegal pharmaceuticals and the like," Lawrence introduced.

"Drug dealer?" Aretha asked.

Sam began to explain. "Not in the purest sense. He sold potentially lethal things like, well, aluminum hydroxide and, more unique to this case, mercury. I found traces on his clothing. Sadly enough he had enough residual on him to be very ill by end of day."

"We questioned his employer to find that he was stealing chemicals—apparently chemicals for making small bombs, lethal tinctures and the like, but more recently mercury. Some was missing on their ledger the day Boyd didn't come back from lunch," Lawrence explained.

"So Boyd was like a mercury dealer," Jim joined in with one of his cruder jokes.

"Who buys mercury?" Marcel asked.

"That's what I wanna know. I'm a Ford man myself," Jim answered.

Sam began explaining again. "We found trace residual on her body, which makes me wonder about the bedding."

"So you think someone bought mercury to kill Harold and put it in his bed?" Marcel asked.

"Who is trying to kill Harold?" Jim asked. "Who is Harold that someone wants him dead in such a King-Henry-the-Eighth kinda way?"

"Yes, we found traces of it on the bottle of wine. Now, that was Harold's bottle. He identified it. There's no way anyone could put mercury dust on the wine bottle knowing Mr. Kitchener would be there to touch it at that time. I'm just not buying that. As I said before, we have no indication that mercury is a party drug of any sort." Sam snickered as if he was the only one who got the joke. He cleared his throat. "My guess is the mercury was dissipated into the air somehow—throughout that entire condo. My guess is someone is killing him softly—with or without a song." Sam chuckled again at his own lame joke.

The others just looked at each other. "So you think Boyd made the mercury sale to the person trying to kill Harold? Then that person killed Boyd so he wouldn't ID them. Then that person tried to kill Harold but killed Victoria instead," Marcel suggested. "Maybe that's not how it went. Maybe Boyd and Victoria just accidently touched their faces and mouths with something from work, or somebody else touched them on the mouth with this aluminum whatever?"

"Oh no, it was orally induced."

"Yeah, there is no way somebody kissed him and did all that," Jim said, pointing at what was left of Boyd's oral cavity.

"I'm just sayin' however they did it, they got acid in Jameson's mouth. I doubt if he just put it in there himself. Ms. Victoria didn't fight the painful process because of the Rohypnol. Boyd had nothing as a buffer except a burger so, yeah, he felt it immediately and shows many internal and external signs of vexing," Sam went on.

"There goes your acid indigestion theory." Jim snickered. Lawrence clearly tried to fight the urge but gave into it. Aretha shook her head at the two men and then glared at her partner, Marcel, daring him to even break a smile.

"So you think we have the same killer? And, if so, we need to find out why she needed to get her hands on mercury if she already had something so deadly in her possession."

"Oh, Aretha, now tell me how you deduced that it was a woman so quickly," Sam said, sounding impressed.

Aretha continued, "It's like this. Had it been a man, he more than likely would have shot Boyd to kill him quickly. A woman was able to get Boyd to poison himself and did it without sex. Had it been a man, Ms. Victoria here would have been sexed before she died—maybe even with her face eaten off."

"How did you know there was no sex?" Sam asked.

"For one you didn't say there had been. For another, that's how men do business. Did you see any money on him? He'd not gotten paid. She seduced him, sure—killed him before money even changed hands. She wasn't about to have sex with him. I mean, he's no prize. Get real. She used another ploy to get Boyd to poison himself," Aretha added, noting Boyd's obviously less-than-good looks, even on what was left of his face.

"Okay, let's go with the woman theory for the sake of conversation," Jim said, catching on to Aretha's train of thought. "Why would a woman need mercury?"

"Better yet, who was that woman gonna kill using mercury?" Aretha asked him.

"How does one kill with mercury?" Jim pondered aloud.

"Well with mercury, you—" Sam began.

Lawrence touched him lightly on the shoulder to silence him. "Let 'em work. I've seen magic come from this kind of rambling. They'll figure it all out on their own."

"That's probably why he's with you and she's with me," Marcel concurred. "Together they'd be superheroes."

"Slowly, to my understanding," Aretha said, answering the question about how one kills with mercury. "That is, unless she planned to serve up a big honkin' amount of it in the tuna fish. To my understanding, we all eat mercury at some time in our lives, and if we have old fillings, we eat it every day. So, with that said, if she wanted to kill with it and make it look like an accident, she'd have to serve it up slow. However she planned to do it, she'd better planned to do it right. She'd have to be a pro or else she could end up killing herself," Aretha went on. "And it sounds like she's not quite got it; I'm hearing the word 'residual' a lot today."

"Well, I heard dust—rhymes with lust but nobody had sex, right? How does one learn to make mercury dust?"

"She learned it from wherever and from whoever she got that aluminum hydroxide," Aretha answered.

"That's got me thinking that she probably didn't plan to kill Boyd so quickly. I think she knew she'd given him a lethal dose, but I can't imagine that she wanted to leave a body to clean up that way—women are usually neater, aren't they?" Jim said, sounding tongue-in-cheek.

Aretha rolled her eyes. "So, she kills Boyd faster than she planned. Stuff happens, okay, she had to do it. Boyd musta figured out something she didn't want him to know or tell. But she wasn't planning to kill Victoria at all, let alone quickly. She's been too busy trying to kill Harold Kitchener . . . slowly. I think Victoria walked into the cloud of mercury that was already there in Harold's apartment."

"So little Ms. Chemistry Set is screwing up?"

"I'd say so. Then we're just about done here," Jim added.

"Yup. She's screwed up twice; third time's a charm."

Jim and Aretha turned back to Marcel and Lawrence.

"Who'd wanna kill Harold slowly? Are we still talking about a woman?" Lawrence asked, trying to keep up.

"My sister?" Marcel said.

"The dead one?" Jim asked bluntly.

"Jim!" Aretha snapped.

"He brought it up. I'm just asking."

"I've never believed my sister is dead—ever."

"Well, you said Harold has been screaming about being haunted. But maybe it's the roofies, maybe . . ." Aretha started.

"Well, let's see if she's been visiting Harold's place," Jim suggested.

"Yeah, I say we need to do a major once-over of Harold's condo. He's probably got a mercury leak somewhere and some prints."

"Remember, guys, all this is supposition. We've got two dead bodies and in just these few minutes we tied them together in the most bizarre kinda knot," Sam jumped in.

"I say let's just get over there and do some dusting."

"No good, 'cause dusting Harold's place for prints is only gonna bring up Phoebe's prints. She lived there."

"Well, where else is she haunting? Your folks talk about seeing her? Your girlfriend? I'm speaking of the queenie, not the meanie," Aretha blurted.

Jim was all over it. "You dating a queen, DuChamp?"

"No, and"—Marcel glared at Aretha—"no."

"Oh." Jim chuckled. "I was about to hit you up for a loan."

"Not from this queen—get your hat handed to you!" Aretha went on. "She hates men."

"Oh, a meanie queenie. I like that type." Jim laughed.

Chapter 44

"What does it take to get you to call me back?" Denise fussed, standing at Lacy's door.

"Um, when did you call me?" Lacy asked, sounding truly ignorant to the facts.

"I've called you fifty-nine times."

"You lie like a lawyer," Lacy said, bursting into laughter.

"Girl, you are so mean. That is, unless you don't know. Of course you don't know. You don't know anything. All you do is work and hide out on the top of a mountain. It is pretty up here, though." Denise looked around admiringly.

"Don't know what? That I'm the beneficiary of Phoebe's insurance policy? Old news, baby! Besides, I'm not gonna win the case. I'm meeting with the insurance guy, Marcel, and he already told me I don't stand a chance in hell. Besides the fact that I don't want the money, they think there's some kind of fraud or whatever, so that will invalidate the entire thing or something like that."

"Marcel tell you that?"

"No. I just told you his name was Steven—Steven Prophet to be exact. Why on earth did you bring up Marcel?"

"I didn't. You did," Denise said, smiling broadly.

"I did?"

"You said Marcel told you blah blah blah . . . Anyway, none of that matters. Adam Stillberg's sister is dead."

"What?"

"Yeah, girl, she was murdered. Found naked in Harold's bed."

"What? When?"

"Oh my friggin' God, you work at a news station and you don't know anything?"

"I work in the studio. I don't listen to the news. Plus the news talent is weird. Oh my God the stories I could tell you—"

"Lacy! Stay with me!" Denise snapped her fingers. Lacy realized she was rambling. Normally rambling was what Denise did. This was strange. She felt suddenly comfortable with Denise. It was weird. "Adam Stillberg's sister is dead. They found Victoria—his sister—dead in Harold's bed."

"What? Is Harold being charged with anything?"

"No, but he's totally under investigation for all kinds of things—Adam Stillberg too."

"What things?"

"Didn't you know? No, of course you didn't. He and Adam made porn films. Phoebe and Sonja are porn stars. She wanted out and he killed her. That's what the police are thinking, and I think so too." Denise stopped speaking and then burst into laughter before continuing. "Isn't that fuckin' fantastic. Oh my God! That money is as good as yours, girlfriend."

Lacy's mouth dropped open.

"You did know Phoebe did porn, right?" Denise asked while looking over her shoulder into the house to make sure she had indeed put the dogs away as she had said she would. "Girl, you could invite a girl in, make her a sandwich, and learn a few things."

"Oh, I would, Denise, but I've been sick. I've got the flu. You know it's going around."

"What flu?"

"The flu," Lacy said, sounding deadpan and flat. "I've got the flu. Everybody's got the flu. I've got the flu—"

"Uh, I don't have the flu," Denise said before giving Lacy a closer stare. "Girl, you don't got the flu, you got a baby. Stop playin'. You're pregnant. Stop playin'."

"Denise, you're so dumb. Come on in then if you just wanna get sick."

"Your kinda sickness I can handle. You are with chile. Please, remember I am from"—she made quotation marks in the air as she strutted into the house—"the old school, and my grandmamma taught me about reading the signs and um . . ." She touched Lacy's neck. Lacy jumped slightly, as she didn't expect Denise to touch her. "You got an additional little pulse jumping off right about here. You're pregnant."

Denise proceeded to look around Lacy's home. It was her first visit there. Maybe Marcel had told her how beautiful the house was. He was the only one who'd actually been up there. Denise obviously kept in touch with Marcel. He would be a golden source of information for a person like her.

Lacy was confident her home would measure up to anything he might say, so she just kept talking. "Stop it. I'm not!" she protested.

"Okay, well, call me in a week and if I'm not sick then, we'll be through talking about it. Anyway, let me fill you in, okay?"

Lacy flopped down on the sofa and pulled her robe tighter around her. She was freezing. She glanced at the fireplace. There hadn't been a fire in there since Marcel's marvelous one the night they made love. Suddenly, she realized Denise was talking and she forced her mind to come back.

"I think Harold did it."

"What? Why would he kill his girlfriend?"

"Because she wouldn't make porn. Anyway, now that he's out of the way you are back in the running."

"I'm not in the running."

"So you say. Personally I think you should watch yourself. I mean, between Harold, Adam, and Sonja, with her jealous ass, you need to be careful. I've seen them together—cavorting."

"Nobody is cavorting. Plus, Sonja is in Europe and if Phoebe was doing porn we'd all know about it." Lacy thought about her words carefully. This was Denise she was talking to. "Where did you see them? When did Sonja get back? Have you seen any of the movies?"

"Thank you," Denise said, noting that Lacy realized the facts about her talents. "It was not too long after the funeral. I saw Harold talking to Sonja near my cousin's office."

"Your cousin."

"Yes, my cousin. Anyway, they were talking pretty cozy-like and, well, I think they are plotting, and now Victoria is dead, Phoebe is dead . . . You better watch your back before you and your baby end up dead."

"Don't say that, Denise."

"I think you better get Marcel up here to protect you."

"Why are you saying that?" Lacy felt her face grow hot.

"Because I saw you leave together from the funeral and now you are calling everybody Marcel and you're pregnant. Math was never my best subject but I can add this one up. Did you tell your mama about the baby? No, what am I saying? She knows. Didn't you go for Thanksgiving?"

"Yes, I did," Lacy said, thinking again about the hot sex with Marcel in the backyard, and how everyone stared at them when they came back in the house. "And you're wrong."

"And Phoebe told me that Marcel busted your cherry and you have been madly crazy in love with him your whole life."

"Oh my God!" Lacy exploded. "She promised me she would never tell!"

At that Denise burst into laughter. "Seriously, she didn't tell. Winston did."

Lacy groaned loudly. "That's even worse."

"Girl, I'm starving. Ooooh I'm craving Chinese," Denise said, no doubt noticing Lacy's empty take-out container sitting on her desk. "And, yes, I've seen one of the movies," Denise said over her shoulder, heading into Lacy's kitchen.

Chapter 45

"It's Phoebe, I tell ya. She's the one who did this to me," Harold bellowed. "I have been trying to tell people forever that Phoebe is haunting me."

"Harold, stop it, before you end up in the mental ward. We're going to find out how mercury got in your air conditioner duct, okay? But you gotta quit saying it was Phoebe," Marcel explained. "Phoebe is dead."

"You didn't find her body, did you? No! And I have to tell you that she had planned to kill me on that boat! Adam all but told me that. She had an accomplice—Barry somebody. The boat guy . . . Yeah, that fat fuck, she plotted with him to kill me."

"Shut up, Harold!" Marcel growled. Aretha held his arm to calm him.

It was true, Phoebe's prints were all over the condo; that was as expected. But so were Sonja's, Adam's, Victoria's, and a few random ones for good measure, including a few latent prints of Lacy's. Marcel's mind soared when he heard that Lacy's prints were there. He immediately was jealous and jumping to conclusions. It was hard not to imagine the worst with all that filming equipment and other sexual apparatuses.

"When was Lacy at your house?" Aretha asked Harold.

"She wasn't there. Not recently, at least. Not while I was there, anyway, but then who knows what goes on while I'm gone. Apparently a hell of a lot goes on. People try to kill me while I'm gone!"

"Harold, no one was trying to kill you."

"That's a lie. You found the mercury and the roofies. I didn't try to kill myself. I didn't put that shit in my wine. Somebody is trying to kill me. Hey, it probably was Lacy. She and Phoebe probably plotted this whole fuckin' thing to get my money. Yeah, Phoebe would fake her death and then she and Lacy would hook up and enjoy the money."

"Why would Lacy and Phoebe do that?" Marcel asked.

He looked at Marcel strangely. "How should I know? They were probably fucking. Lacy was probably fucking my wife! Like everyone else!" Harold answered.

At that comment Marcel began choking Harold while he lay in the bed. "Shut the fuck up, you lyin', murderous, scum-sucking, bottom-feeding motherfucker!"

They had brought Harold into the hospital for observation after finding the condo contaminated with mercury. Yes, Harold was being killed slowly by the mercury poisoning. It was a death that would never be traced to the root cause, and whoever was killing him was going to get away with it. His merlot bottle was full of Rohypnol. He told the police he only sipped a little at night for his stomach ailment. That was why Victoria went out so quickly. She'd had two of three full glasses.

It was hard to say if the Rohypnol was for him, or if he'd put it there for Victoria. It was suggested that he would drug her and film her during sex. Harold denied even the thought of doing something so foul to Victoria. Yet here he was saying something so foul about Phoebe—which led to Marcel choking him.

Aretha grabbed Marcel to pull him off of Harold, who was howling and baying as if wounded.

Chapter 46

Lacy wasn't sure when the funeral was going to be but she called Harold. She felt badly for treating his feelings as if they were nothing all these weeks. He didn't answer his office phone or his cell. His secretary had said he was out on personal leave for the rest of the month—maybe even until the first of the year.

"Really? Wow."

"Yes, he's had a death in the family," she volunteered.

"Yes, I know. His wife died a few months ago."

"Okay," the girl said, as if that were old news.

"It was hard on him," Lacy defended to the rude-sounding receptionist.

"Yeah, I should guess so, and now with his girlfriend dying. They found her naked in his bed—dead—last week, and whoever killed Victoria tried to kill Harold too."

"What? Are you kidding me?"

"No, I'm not, and the police are investigating it. They think it was murder," she said. "It's in the paper, so I'm not telling you anything you couldn't find out if you knew anything about the news," she added as if covering her butt. It was obvious she had no idea that Lacy worked at a news station and that the man she loved worked in homicide. Of course, she was pissed whenever she thought about the fact that it wasn't from Marcel that she got this information.

"Really?" Lacy responded. Her mind ran amuck. She even found herself thinking about the insurance policy, which was all but dead to her. She'd not heard a word since standing Steven Prophet up. It was almost as if that whole situation was being handled without her. But now with just the hint that Harold could have been the object of a real killer, Lacy started thinking about the situation concerning the money again. She felt as obtuse as the people she worked with—just so out of touch. She felt untouchable sometimes. Life had become so surreal—just like the life of her alter ego, Queen Hynata.

"What if I don't have the flu?" she asked herself for the first time aloud. She'd not wanted to face what her body was doing. She'd not wanted to think that her super-light (more like simply spotting) periods could be caused by something more than stress.

After hanging up with the receptionist, she called the station to verify the news she'd heard. She could have looked it up on the Internet, but she was already on the phone. Doris, on the other hand, looked it up in the news station's daily news archives. "Yep. Victoria Stillberg. She's dead. They are suspecting foul play. She was found naked in Harold Kitchener's bed. Didn't his wife just die? Is this guy a lady killer or what?"

"Has Harold been indicted?"

"No. But it hasn't been released how she died for sure. They are just calling it suspected foul play. But he's been taken to the hospital for possible mercury poisoning. What's that all about? Anyway, you coming in tomorrow?" she asked, changing the subject abruptly as if they'd been discussing the weather.

"Why wouldn't I?" Lacy asked her.

"Oh, just something I heard."

"What'd you hear?"

"I heard that you're sick or something."

"No. I'm fine. Who told you I was sick?"

"Just heard it."

"My goodness, the stuff you hear around there." Lacy balked before hanging up.

She pondered calling Denise, but wasn't sure she was up to the information overload. Nonetheless, curiosity had her cat and was choking it to death. Gathering what she needed for a down-the-hill run, she got the car ready. The dogs jumped in as together they planned first a Chinese food run and then maybe some donuts via Harold's condo. Perhaps he would be there and Lacy would be able to talk to him about what was going on. She was ready to listen now—with her mind and ears open.

Having forgotten her phone, she went back in the house to find it. For such an expensive item she was surely careless with it. Finding it tucked deep in the sofa cushions she shoved it deep in her pockets and headed back toward the door. Swinging open the door to leave again, she found two police officers standing there. It was obvious they were cops by the "unobvious" undercover attire—tan trench coats and shiny black shoes.

One was a tall, bear-like black officer, and the other a shorter white one who resembled an older and scruffier Brad Pitt. "Ms. Durham, we'd like to talk to you," the white officer said, inviting himself in with his eyes by probing over her shoulder immediately. His eyes settled on hers. "We'd like to come in." He smiled.

Lacy backed away from the door and allowed the men to come in. "What's wrong?" she asked, thinking immediately of Marcel. "Is this about Marcel DuChamp?"

"Oh, so you know?" Jim said before Lawrence nudged him hard.

"What?"

The tall man glared at the shorter one before he spoke. "No, it's about Harold Kitchener."

"What about that guy? Are you here to serve me with a lawsuit or something? See, I was just getting ready to take care of that when his girlfriend was murdered," Lacy said, before hearing her words and feeling instant regret.

The men looked at each other again and then back at her. "No."

"Good, because I've told that jerk time and time again, I don't need the money! I don't want the money! And—"

"And we think somebody may still be trying to kill you for the money! We think someone tried to kill Mr. Kitchener and they may be trying to kill you."

"What!"

"We'd like your permission to search your house."

"For what?"

"For a deadly chemical . . . possibly in your air ducts."

"My ducts! I just had my ducts done about a month ago. Oh my God! Why would anybody want to hurt me?"

Chapter 47

Lacy called and knocked, banged and screamed for Dave. His car was in his driveway so she knew he had to be around. He wasn't out walking the cliffs, nor was he answering his house phone. She'd not seen him since her Thanksgiving vacation at her folks'. He dropped off the dogs and Pete and left without much delay. Lacy didn't ask, but she figured Raven had returned.

Maybe she has a car. Maybe she and Dave are in the city. Fine, Lacy thought, suddenly feeling a little left out. She needed him right now. The police had searched her home for a chemical that could have killed her. They found nothing, but just the thought disturbed her that someone had actually tried to kill Harold, and just because her name was on a paper she somehow could be involved. She was so out of the loop—so far removed from any of this. Why did it seem as though she had tripped and fallen right smack dab in the middle of all of this mess?

She needed to talk to Dave; he'd calm her down, he'd bring her thinking back to where it should be—*in reality and out of the movie theatre!*

But, no, he wasn't home. He was running around with this *Raven* woman. Lacy was jealous, but, allowing herself to get a grip for a second, she had to accept that Raven seemed to be the woman for Dave. He was clearly taken with her, although he hadn't talked about her much. All Lacy knew was the name Raven, which to her smacked of a pseudonym. *Why the mystery, little girl?* Lacy asked herself while still pressing her face in the window. It was just so strange for Dave not to be home on a Saturday.

Maybe she'd come to take Dave for granted. She'd come to depend on him too much for companionship. He was, after all, all she really had for a friend. "That's not true, Lace, you have Denise," she mumbled before realizing she'd called herself Lace. Her mind went back to the night at her parents'. She'd been fighting that memory since that night. She fought any thoughts that attempted to put reasoning behind this craziness that she and Marcel had started. It was obvious that what they were doing was making no sense. It wasn't as if they'd talked about it, or planned to take it further.

It was just situational as far as she was concerned. If Phoebe hadn't died it may not have even happened. "I know that for a fact. If Phoebe were still alive, Marcel wouldn't be thinking about me," she said, trying to convince herself that someone could make love to her the way Marcel did and feel nothing for her.

She was going to head to her parents' in a couple of days for Christmas. She hoped Marcel wasn't going to be seeing his parents. She couldn't face seeing him again. Especially now with this investigation going on, she felt accused and distrusted. Maybe Marcel was suspecting her of being a part of all this craziness with Phoebe's death. She couldn't believe the police actually searched her house. Did Marcel send them to do it? The short guy kept saying things that sounded as if Marcel knew about this search. She was fuming. Why she was angry with Marcel she wasn't sure . . . Oh, yeah, she was! She missed him and wanted to see him. She wanted his phone number to call him. She was frustrated beyond belief. She wanted to eat herself silly and then cry herself to sleep!

Denise had called later, after the police and their team left, to tell her that Harold was in the hospital for mercury poisoning. He was going to survive and that was a good thing, of course, but when Lacy told Denise about the search of her house, Denise grew worried. "Girl, somebody doesn't want you or him to get that money. I'm telling you, you better get Marcel up there with you. I'm not kidding." Denise then began to attempt some rational thought. "Maybe they're trying to kill off the popular people from our school. Nah, can't be that, or Victoria wouldn't have gotten killed, and, come to think about it, you're not popular, either. Maybe you're right—yeah, you're safe and I should be worried—not!" She was being sarcastic. "Stop being stupid! You could be in danger. Hell, you are in danger!"

"The police were just here. You are amazing, Denise. You really do think you know everything, and maybe you do. But the one thing you've got wrong is that, Denise, nobody is trying to kill me," Lacy had assured her. "And Marcel would be a horrible bodyguard," she barked without thinking or regretting the words. Dense was quiet and then changed the subject to something lighter.

But then, that night, she got two hang-ups on the phone from blocked numbers. She was terrified being there alone. She found herself loading her gun and bringing in her dogs for the night. She was terrified.

I can't live like that. I can't be living in fear, she thought now, accepting that she was truly afraid and wanted Dave to be home—like now. She didn't know what Dave could do, but at least she needed to bring him into the loop. He needed to know there was a possible killer on the loose. "Maybe the killer was trying to kill Harold," Lacy said aloud. "Wait, stop it. Nobody is trying to kill anybody! If someone was trying to kill me, they would have found mercury in my house yesterday. There have been no attempts on my life! Calm down, Lacy! Harold is not me. Harold has hurt a lot of people and it doesn't surprise me that someone is trying to kill him. It probably has nothing to do with Phoebe's death." Lacy knocked on Dave's door again.

She thought about Denise's last words. "You're being foolish if you don't see this the way it is, Lacy," Denise had said right before she hung up. "You better get a buddy up there on that hill!"

And so here she was at Dave's door. "I've got a buddy," she fussed, knocking on Dave's door again, a little harder now. He needed to know that maybe Phoebe had been murdered, and that somebody could be hanging around with something bad planned for her too.

Just then Dave arrived. He was driving a car Lacy didn't recognize. He obviously didn't see her as he quickly jumped out and went around to the passenger side of the car. The woman stepped out. Her dark hair was up in a bun and her face was covered in several bandages. She didn't quite look like a mummy, but it was pretty close, as far as Lacy was concerned. She could hear Dave helping her into the side door. She stepped around the house.

"Dave!" she screeched.

Both Dave and the woman were startled. She could see it in the way the woman jumped. She had on sunglasses, so Lacy couldn't see her eyes, but she could guess they were widened by the startle.

"Lacy! What . . . what are you doing here?"

"I was just here to see if you wanted to walk the dogs. But you weren't here . . . obviously," Lacy stated matter-of-factly. "No, I'm lying. The police were at my house yesterday. Did they come by here? Did they?"

"Yes, umm no, they didn't, or maybe I missed them. I wasn't home. Go on inside, Raven." Dave ushered inside the woman who stood staring at Lacy as if she'd seen a ghost.

"So that's Raven. What happened to her?" Lacy asked.

"She fell and—"

"Again! When you met her she had fallen. Boy, she's accident prone." Lacy laughed nervously.

"Well I guess so," he said with the same amount of nervousness.

Lacy could see he was growing tense, and the situation was getting far too weird. "Well, tell her I hope she gets better. She's in great hands and well . . ." Lacy shrugged. "I hope to meet her soon."

"I hope the two of you can meet one day too."

Lacy turned to leave, but just then Oz the dog came from his adventure snooping around the inside of Dave's house. He had something in his teeth. Retrieving it, Lacy could see it was a woman's scarf. Opening it, she noticed the monogrammed initials PD. Immediately she thought of Phoebe. She stared at the initials for a long time. When she got ready to hand it back to Dave she saw that he stood mortified and stiff. "I'm sorry, Dave. I can replace the scarf. It's hers, right?"

Dave snatched the scarf. "No! Yes!"

"What does PD stand for?"

"Patty Duke. It's a famous scarf. I got it at a party. Lacy, what did the police want?"

"They were looking for mercury in my air ducts. Isn't that the craziest thing? My friend . . . I told you about my friend. Her husband ended up in the hospital because of mercury poisoning and so they were worried about me. Why would they be worried about me, Dave?"

The silence between them was thick. "Because you're Queen Hynata and they'd hate for something to happen to you, silly goose! Lacy, they came by because you know that man. You are involved with him indirectly through this insurance mess. That's why. But stop worrying. The queen will get her cool mil and life on the hill will be good again. You act like that kind of money just comes with no problems."

"You are so crazy . . ." Lacy chuckled. "Yes, you're right. It's because I'm queen. It's because I'm connected. Thank you. You're so good at bringing me down from the crazy skies of make-believe. Oh, and about the scarf. My friend, the one who died, her initials were PD, for Phoebe DuChamp. The scarf made me think of her again. It's hard not to think about her with all this mess. So much reminds me of her these days."

"I'm sure it does."

"I just miss her. I mean, I know we had started drifting apart near the end but, lately, I just feel really close to her. I feel sometimes like she's watching me," Lacy confessed for the first time—even to herself. She'd had dreams of Phoebe. She felt her presence in her home—smelled her perfume. Lacy thought she might be going a little nutty—kind of like Harold. But, then again, she chalked it up to delayed grief. Marcel's presence in her life wasn't helping. She had no one to talk to about Marcel and her feelings about him. She needed Phoebe right now. She needed to talk to Phoebe about her love for Marcel. "She was like a sister to me," Lacy added.

"Well, you never know," Dave said, stroking the scarf. "Maybe one day you and Raven will get close like that."

"Wow, you talk like she's gonna live here forever."

"I'd like that."

"Well, as soon as she gets better, bring her by. I'd love to finally meet her."

"I think you'll be pleasantly surprised at how well you two hit it off."

"If you like her, Dave, then I already do too."

Chapter 48

Lacy tried to put everything else out of her mind. She went to work as if it were a normal day. She put on her queen mindset and, after parking her car, entered the building, strolled past Doris with a normal hello, and down the elevator she went. She'd gotten there early and the afternoon weather shoot had just ended. Everyone was regrouping for the newscast that would be filming in about a half hour. Then they would air Queen Hynata for the children. She grabbed a donut out of the open box and wolfed it down before making a quick trip to the bathroom.

The door opened and the weather girl entered. She stared at her before entering the stall. Lacy could see her reflection in the mirror. Lacy knew her makeup was perfect—she had paid nearly $200 at the mall to make sure it would be—so what was this weather girl staring at so hard?

"What!" Lacy finally snapped at her.

"You look different somehow," she said. "Oh, and Gary told me to give you this," she then said before handing her a list of revisions for the week's script. "Oh, and we're having a holiday party on Friday before everybody goes nuts for X-mas."

"X-mas? Can't you say Christmas?" Lacy asked sarcastically.

"Sure, I can," was all the girl answered.

There was a long pause before the girl took a deep breath and continued to speak. Lacy's donut was turning and returning—not settling well at all. *Maybe Gary poisoned it.* Her mind jumped.

"Are you feeling all right?" the girl asked.

Lacy viciously ripped off a paper towel before wetting it to cool off her face. "I ate one of those donuts. Are we using a new bakery? I don't think their donuts are fresh," Lacy answered.

"I've been eating donuts all morning . . . Lots. They're fresh," the skinny weather girl said, brushing her fine blond hair out of her eyes and backward on her head. She wore her hair in a simple '70s hippie kind of style. It wasn't very contemporary but, then again, neither was that fringed leather jacket and satchel bag she carried, or those bell-bottoms she sported from time to time, or those short skirts and go-go boots. This chick was a throwback for sure. Suddenly, with a violent urgency, Lacy darted into a stall, sick to her stomach.

"Yup, I just figured out what it is that's different about you." The weather girl continued to talk as Lacy vomited. "It's your skin. Boy, your skin has really cleared up pretty. Not that it was bad skin or anything, but you look more, you know, ethnic looking now . . . Dark." The weather girl giggled, finally entering the next stall and doing her business.

Lacy had been noticing annoying dark blotches on her neck and chest area, but she just let it go.

"And," the weather girl continued, talking from inside her stall before flushing and exiting, "you have boobs now," she added. "Not that I'm into boobs on other women but I do notice things like that, especially on a skinny girl like you." She washed her hands.

In the stall, Lacy looked down and touched her increasingly tender heavy breasts squeezed into that 34B bra that she wore. She had imagined that the bra had somehow shrunk on laundry day.

"You're preggers," the weather girl blurted.

"What?" Lacy gasped, catching her breath long enough to respond after quickly upchucking one more time. She used a toilet cover to wipe her mouth, and then flushed it down.

"Yup. I may be wrong about the weather sometimes," she understated, "and that's only sometimes, but I'm never wrong about some things and this is one of those things. I'm never wrong about pregnancy."

How could she have just ignored it for so long? Why did she ignore it until others noticed? Did Marcel know? Had he seen it too and that's why he stared so hard? Was Denise right? Was her neck throbbing all over the place? Lacy grabbed at her throat as if she could feel anything other than her own racing heartbeat. Just then she looked up to see an e.p.t. stick sticking over the top of the stall.

"Yeah, I keep 'em in my purse—before you even ask. I know, it's weird, but just go ahead and piss on it. You can thank me later."

Hesitating momentarily while thinking about things— mostly how eccentric the weather girl really was—Lacy then snatched the early pregnancy test from her hand and urinated on it. "You better be wrong!" she yelled from inside the stall.

Chapter 49

Lacy sat nervously biting her nails with her bare butt against the rough paper sheet that covered the small table, while she waited for Dr. Minion. She had taken off early. It was the first sick time she had taken since working there. She blamed it on ozone depletion, saying that it had affected her sinuses. It was easy to believe. No one seemed to really care anyway, or so it seemed. Even her boss only half looked up when she told him she'd be leaving early.

"Well, queenie . . ." Dr. Minion began, teasing her as he often did. He had been her doctor since her childhood. He was a portly black man, about sixty-five. He had a face like a teddy bear and Lacy always felt comfortable with him, even with him being the only one who knew she lost her virginity to Marcel DuChamp. Now, he was about to know Marcel was the father of her baby. "It's not the flu, but then, I'm sure you knew that," he chuckled. "You're quite pregnant." He sat down on the stool beside the table she sat on. Her back felt the draft coming in from the opening in the paper gown, and she shook from a sudden chill as he spoke directly to her. "You are going to be a mother." He chuckled, aiming for comic relief, which didn't come. "That's if you want to be. I have a friend who's an obstetrician who can take over your care while you're pregnant. You know I just handle colds and aches and pains and . . ." Dr. Minion was speaking in a lighthearted tone, but stopped suddenly, noticing Lacy's facial expression changing dramatically.

Lacy began to cry. "It's Marcel's baby. You remember him. The boy—"

"The boy next door?" Dr. Minion asked. "DuChamp's kid," he added. Dr. Minion knew everybody.

"Well, he's far from next door now. He's a police officer now. He's all grown up," Lacy said, thinking of Marcel.

"I see." Dr. Minion was sounding like a father now.

"Well, it was after the funeral. Remember, Phoebe died. . . ."

"Yes," he said. "That long ago, oh my. Lie down," he instructed. He put on his stethoscope. "That long ago, we can probably hear a heartbeat by now!"

"Already? Oh my God. What should I do?"

"Have you talked to your parents?"

"No. I haven't. I'm not sure what to tell them."

"Tell them that I think they are about to have a couple of grandchildren."

"What?"

Dr. Minion handed her the earpieces to the stethoscope for her to listen. He moved the device from one side of her belly to the other. "Hear it?" he asked. Lacy nodded. He moved the device higher. "Hear that?"

She nodded.

"I think we got two babies in there. I think we got a little twin action."

Lacy began to cry again.

Chapter 50

The next morning Ray and Sarah woke early and had their coffee, quietly as usual, sitting together, reading the paper undisturbed . . . as usual. Their life was a lot quieter now. Not that Lacy had been much trouble growing up, but she was a loud kid. They missed having her around. They really did. She was their baby, their only child. Clumsy and awkward, whiney, and curious, she was always in the way; she took up a lot of their energies. They adored all those traits, though, and at about eleven A.M., the door opened and there she stood, exhibiting a couple of them.

"What a surprise," Sarah said, looking Lacy over, immediately noticing even more changes in her appearance. She'd seen the start of the changes during the Thanksgiving dinner. She had a strange feeling she knew what those changes meant, but Lacy hadn't said anything and she hadn't pushed her. But the flush on Marcel's and her cheeks when they came from that little trash run said all she didn't want to hear. "Your jeans are awfully tight there, honey," she said.

"Sarah, is that all you can see?" Ray, Lacy's father, asked, jumping up to give her a tight squeeze. He stroked her hair.

"And gonna get tighter, Daddy," Lacy mumbled into his chest. He smelled like Bengay and coffee.

"What's that?" Sarah asked, overhearing her.

Lacy took a deep breath before pushing her father back and standing straight and tall in front of her parents. "I'm pregnant. It's Marcel's baby. I've decided not to tell him and I want your support in my decision," she announced in one breath. "I'm going to fight harder to get the money Phoebe left me, because I'm going to quit the television station and the show, because I don't want to be on TV all big and fat and—"

"Oh my God. You'll do no such thing," her mother interjected, taking on a slightly irritated tone. "It's not like they're going to make the little cartoon you play all fat and everything. Nobody even sees you!"

"Motherrrrr," Ray began.

"It'll be all right, Mother. I want to do this. I've been thinking, ya know. I could change careers. I could always write another book and—" Lacy tried hard not to react to the 'fat' comments.

"You will not quit your job. Do you know how expensive a baby is? No, you don't. After taxes you think you're gonna get far off a million dollars? No. It's only gonna be about seventy-five thousand. You nearly make that on your job." Sarah smacked her lips and turned her head away. Sarah knew she was horrible at math, but she hoped Lacy understood her point. She was surprised at her own words and apparently Lacy was too, and began to laugh. Sarah had done her homework on Lacy's life. She knew about the insurance policy—hell, who didn't?

"Well, then, I guess I better rethink this, considering there are twins in there," Lacy said, pointing at her belly.

At that Sarah's mouth dropped open. She looked over at Ray, whose mouth had done the same.

Chapter 51

That was easy enough, Lacy thought as she drove into work the following Monday after spending the rest of the week with her folks. She was actually pretty excited about the holiday coming up. She couldn't wait to eat all she wanted, not that she hadn't been doing that lately—a lot—but this time she was going to do with intent, knowing her mother was preparing all her favorites, just because she was pregnant. "This is gonna be great!" she chuckled. "Today is great!"

She was feeling euphoric and it wasn't just because she was pregnant, or because she was pregnant with twins. It was that she was pregnant with Marcel's twins. She giggled again.

Pulling into the parking stall she suddenly felt the growing anxiety. *Ugh, my coworkers. What will they say? Sure, the wacko weather girl knew but who believes her? She's always wrong about stuff,* Lacy thought, parking her car in her stall.

Stepping out of her car she spied Doris just arriving as well. She smiled. Doris smiled back and headed for the elevator as usual. Lacy let out her bated breath. She didn't know what to expect from her coworkers. It was a silly feeling she had that they would be somehow different.

Stepping out of the elevator onto the floor, she looked around out of reflex for Gary. He'd been back on the job for a few weeks now after his lengthy suspension. He'd been detained by the police that night and was unable to call in the next day. He was suspended. Once the producer realized why he'd missed work it made it even worse. Lacy was sure everybody knew about it by now. She'd heard about it secondhand and it was her own business.

He noticed her. A questioning frown came over his brow as if he saw something different in her, or maybe he was just wondering why she was staring at him so hard.

Finally reaching her desk she found three messages from Denise requesting an immediate lunch date. "That woman is a soothsayer for sure," Lacy mumbled, accepting that somehow Denise already knew.

To her surprise, Gary eased over to her desk. She hoped it was to talk about some sound issues for today's filming. He was smiling. "Hey," he said, sounding clean and sober.

"Hi." She began fiddling with her notes and message pad.

"You look great," he said. "Change something?"

"No, Gary. I didn't."

"How about dinner?" he asked.

She looked at him sternly. "No. No dinner . . . ever again."

"Come on, legs—"

"And my name is not legs. It's Lacy. Lacy Durham. I'm a national bestselling author. I'm a successful voice-over actress for the popular cartoon character Queen Hynata. I'm a homeowner with good credit. I love my parents and I'm pregnant."

Gary's mouth dropped open at her last statement. "Oh my God, Lacy, I'm sorry. I mean, I never meant to . . . I mean . . . Is it too late to get an abortion?"

Glancing around, Lacy saw that they had a full audience now. "It's not your baby, Gary. I would never have your baby! It's the baby of the man I love!" Lacy began searching madly for the crushed flower she'd pressed in her notebook. She began tossing things off her desk wildly in her search. She couldn't stop. She was growing hysterical. "The man who got me the flowers, Gary. The man who isn't afraid to show that he cares about me!" Her face was on fire.

"Calm down, Lacy! It's okay if you wanna have my baby. You don't have to lie about it," Gary went on. "You're not the first to get knocked up by me and wanna keep the baby and . . ."

Lacy resisted slapping his face. Instead she grabbed her purse and tore for the elevator. She had to get out of there quickly. Once she reached the outside she wasn't sure she wanted to ever go back. One thing she was sure of, however; she had to find a Chinese food place quickly!

But first she had one more stop to make.

Chapter 52

Marcel had a two-week suspension for his hospital stunt. It was going to be a great opportunity for him to work with Steven on the case. Steven had told him last time they spoke—awhile ago now, it seemed—that he hadn't gotten very far with Barry Nugent. Marcel now knew Barry was missing. Conferring with Jim and Lawrence he found out that Barry was dead. "I think Harold and whoever else plotted this whole boat thing. Barry musta known about it and that's why they killed him. Then Harold tried to double cross and therefore he had to go," Marcel told Aretha. Aretha decided to continue working with him on this case. Marcel was running out of time before they closed the case and he couldn't let that happen.

"Captain said he heard from the insurance company. It wasn't Steven Prophet but, like, Steven's boss or whatever. They're gonna turn in their report. Apparently Steven dropped the ball. I couldn't get any answers."

"Well I'll go do some snooping around. I don't believe Steven would let me down like this."

"Not everybody believes there is more to this than meets the eye."

"But there is!"

"Not from an insurance viewpoint. The bottom line, Marcel, is that your sister died. Her insurance company has to pay off. Now the rest, that's where we do our jobs, but they have to do theirs."

"You don't get it. Harold is already in the hospital. Somebody already knows the outcome of this case and they are trying to change it."

"The other person who would benefit from Harold being dead is Lacy Durham. Is that what you're trying to say?"

Marcel stared at Aretha. It was, but it wasn't. He couldn't believe that Lacy would kill for the money she claimed she wanted no part of. "No. I don't believe it. I—"

"Marcel, I've never known you to not go with your gut instincts. I've never known you to be seduced by love." Aretha then smiled. "But, then again, I've never known you to be in love."

"Aretha, if this is love, then it sucks. I'm not thrilled with it at all. My brain don't wanna work anymore. My heart—"

"Aches, yeah, I know the feeling," Aretha said, smiling. "Look, if we put our heads together we can find someone else who would benefit from Harold being dead. Let's look at the facts. First, your sister was in a horrible life—that's assuming she didn't want to do those movies," Aretha said, clearly treading lightly. It took a couple of orderlies to get Marcel off of Harold, and she obviously didn't want to have to fight him over the same topic. "So she tries to kill Harold by rigging a boat job with the help of Barry Nugent. Okay, so things go wrong and she's killed instead—"

"But—"

"Let me finish, Marcel. She's killed, okay, so she's dead now, and Harold thinks he's gonna get some money since she's insured up the ass, okay? But no, she insured her best bud, Lacy Durham. Nobody knew Lacy was her best bud, but hey . . . we don't know everything sometimes. So anyway, Lacy is named beneficiary.

Harold is not happy, gets his attorney involved, Adam Stillberg. Adam is a slime ball and, from what I've discovered . . ." Again Aretha was treading lightly. Marcel had to figure she'd watched one of the movies. Any good cop would have watched the movies. There had to have been clues there. Marcel, however, couldn't bring himself to watch any of them. "He shared a passion for the bright lights of show business."

"What?"

"Yeah. So, Adam and Harold know that Lacy could actually win. Slim chance, but she could win all this money once people realize that Harold was using Phoebe for gain—as a matter of fact, he was planning to film on the boat the day it went up. Okay, so, my thoughts are that maybe Harold decides to do a little acting himself by making it look like he's being stalked by the ghost of your sister, and, in the end, murdered—or at least attempted to be—by Lacy Durham."

"That makes no sense."

"When I spoke to Harold—"

"When did you talk to Harold?"

"After you kicked his ass, I went back to the hospital and talked to the guy. Anyway, he told me Phoebe always came to him in the dreams as a redhead. He said he now believes it was Lacy Durham."

"He's fulla shit."

"I agree, but at least talk to Lacy. Get some confirmations and stuff. I mean, everybody is dropping like flies and she's got no alibi for any of it. She doesn't even have an alibi for the night your sister died!"

"Nobody does! I mean, for that matter, I don't."

"Yes, you do. You were working. Now take off the rose-colored glasses and go talk to Lacy Durham. If you don't, I will."

"Shit," Marcel groaned.

Chapter 53

Adam walked in from the funeral. He couldn't believe he'd buried his baby sister. She was his only relative and now she was gone. He loosened his tie thinking about his life and how that damned Harold had taken the last of what he had on earth from him. He knew what killed Victoria was intended to kill Harold. Sonja and Phoebe were vindictive bitches, but neither really had anything against Victoria. They pitied her. They both knew what Harold was going to do to her.

He'd taken Phoebe's insecurities and turned her into a whore. He'd taken Sonja's love for Phoebe and turned it into an obsession. Harold had taken Adam's legal know-how and greed and turned him into a criminal.

Victoria had broken up with Harold. She'd called him right after she told Harold to fuck off. She called Adam and told him that she was through being with Harold, because she'd seen the movies and didn't want anything to do with that kind of perversion. She'd called him a pervert. She'd said that he and Harold were perverts. "What were you doing naked in his bed? Damn you, Victoria. Now you're dead. I tried to tell you it was time to let Harold go. Why didn't you listen to me? Now you're dead. Which one of those bitches killed you?"

Adam pondered the progression of events. *Why would Sonja want to kill Harold before he got the money? If she killed Harold before he got the money, then Lacy would get it by default. If Lacy got it, Phoebe would have to kill her to get it but, then again, that's what Phoebe wanted to do from the start—wasn't it? That makes no sense. Phoebe killing Lacy makes no sense. Maybe Sonja was right and Phoebe and Lacy were in cahoots. Maybe that bitch Lacy is in on it. Maybe she's playing us all and she's in on it with those other two crazy bitches and fucking Marcel right into compliance,* he thought. Adam tried to remember Lacy from school. She was always the quiet one. His mother used to warn him about quiet girls. "They are up to the devil's work," she'd say. Adam smiled at the thought of his mother. He cried for weeks after she died. Apparently his father's heart broke too, as he died within the year.

"And now Victoria is gone. Damn Harold. Damn Phoebe. Damn Sonja—fuck 'em all," Adam barked, confused and ready to be done with this whole thing. "Nothing is worth my sister's life. Not even a million dollars."

Adam sat down at his desk. His head was pounding. Just then the redheaded woman walked into the office. "You always come here when you're unhappy. It's too bad you don't have a warm home and someone to care for you."

Without speaking to her, he reached over and took his bottle of aspirin in his hand. "My head is killing me," he said aloud before opening the bottle and popping a couple of the pills into his mouth.

"I could be that woman for you, Adam."

"I thought you hated redheads. Why are you wearing that wig?"

"I could be the woman you want. We could just get the money and leave."

"I don't want to talk about money right now. Dammit! My sister just died! Don't you care?" Adam pulled out his gun and pointed it at her. She gasped. "My sister just died. Did you kill her?"

"Adam, of course not. Think about it. Ask yourself, where's Phoebe?"

"What?"

"I haven't seen her since right before Victoria was murdered. She said she was going to get things straight with Harold. She was going to expose us to Harold and then to the police."

"Well good. You need some exposure. I always said you'd do well with a little more exposure." Adam was being sarcastic.

"What? Are you two plotting against me? I know you've always loved Phoebe."

"You're crazy." Reaching over for his bottled water, he finally took a swig to swallow the pills.

"I'm crazy enough to kill—again," she said.

Adam's eyes widened as he slowly lowered the water bottle. "What?"

"I'm wearing this wig so that anybody who sees me won't know me. They may think I'm somebody else. I mean, your sister just died. I could be anybody stopping by to pay condolences, like maybe even Lacy Durham. I wore it when I dumped Barry Nugent's body in the ocean. I wore this wig when I killed the man who sold me the mercury. I was going to kill Lacy and then leave the country with Phoebe wearing it, so that people would think that Lacy and her lover—some blond chick who looked like Marilyn Monroe—left the country. But, no; Phoebe changed the plan and stopped me from killing Lacy with the mercury in her air duct, sooo . . . I got angry and told Harold that Phoebe was alive and what she was planning."

"Harold knows? How long has he known?"

"Long enough for you to give him an alibi when I put poison in the wine bottle that apparently your little sister drank instead of Harold. He wasn't supposed to need an alibi—he was supposed to just report the poisoned wine and mercury to the police as if Lacy had been slowly trying to kill him, but anyway . . . So much for the double-triple-dipple-cross, eh? So anyway, all that fell apart when that nosy insurance guy tried to take my picture and I had to kill him—at least I hope I did. I was in a rush because, well, because somebody pulled up. But the more I thought about things, the more I realized that this plan isn't going to work. It's just hell trying to create accidents when life's destiny starts fighting you. So forget the accidental. I'm just gonna straight out kill your ass!"

Within what seemed like seconds, his throat began to burn. He took another swig, which didn't seem to help. His throat and tongue were on fire. He clawed at his throat as if to attempt to pull the fire from inside but it was to no avail. He dropped the gun.

The last thing he saw was the barrel of a .22 pointed at him. "Good-bye, Adam," she said. "Oh, and yes, a million dollars was worth it—to me."

Chapter 54

"I saw a tall redheaded woman running that way," one of the witnesses declared.

Marcel looked at Aretha, who shook her head as if to urge him not to jump to conclusions. Adam Stillberg was dead. He'd been shot in the chest twice with a small-caliber weapon much like the .22 he saw at Lacy's place the first time he visited there.

His feet were like lead when he, Aretha, Jim, and Lawrence headed up to Lacy's place. He needed the backup because technically he was suspended. Plus, he knew Lacy would bolt if cornered by two strangers. At least he assumed she would—all criminals did.

The door opened to find Lacy with a large tub of ice cream in her hand. It was from the Chez Ice Palace, the fancy-schmancy ice cream place downtown. The line was always hella long and so Marcel hadn't been there in ages. She had a tablespoon in her hand as she stared at the gang of cops at her door. Marcel had never seen her eyes so bright, her skin so silky, her smile so full of life, and her face . . .

"Man, you've gotten fat," he said before he could catch himself.

As if a needle over a record, the moment changed and suddenly all eyes were on him. "Sorry," he said.

"Lacy Durham, we just need to ask to see your gun," Aretha said.

"My gun?" she asked.

"Lacy, Adam Stillberg was killed this afternoon. A redheaded woman was seen leaving the scene—running. He was shot with a twenty-two. You have a twenty-two and—"

"And how do you know I have a twenty-two? Did you go snooping around my kitchen while you were here?" Lacy asked. Marcel could see her emotions rising instantly.

"Can we see your gun?" Aretha repeated.

Lacy stood out of the way and allowed everyone entrance except Marcel. Him she blocked at the door. "It's by my sofa. I had it out the other night when you guys scared me shitless thinking someone was trying to kill *me*," she yelled over her shoulder sarcastically. She turned back to Marcel.

"See, Marcel, it's like this. They thought maybe somebody might be trying to kill me. But I told them they were crazy because nobody cared enough about me to do that. Nobody was thinking about me or my feelings or anything," she growled. "But then that night, I got scared. I actually thought, hey, maybe they were right. So I got out my gun and slept with it by myself because I was *alone* and scared."

"Where were you today, Lace?" Marcel answered, trying to keep his cool.

"Today, at work, I was humiliated by another group of people who couldn't give a shit about me, and I went to get Chinese food—which is all gone!" she yelled out as if maybe they were noticing the containers and looking for leftovers. "And I stood in line for this biggo tub of ice cream for over a damn hour. I'm sure I was there until at least five-thirty . . . You can ask the clerk. Oh, and I used my credit card because that shit's expensive—but I'm worth it. I'd offer you some but there's only enough for the three of us!"

"Three?" Marcel asked, sounding confused but knowing she was being sarcastic.

"The gun is clean. Hasn't been fired in—" Jim said, approaching the door.

"Ever! The gun's never been fired," Lacy confirmed, glaring at the gun in Jim's hands and then at him and then back at Marcel. "I can't believe you came here to accuse me of killing Adam Stillberg. For what, Marcel? Money? I told you I didn't want that money or need that money. I have all I will ever need here in this house with me. Hell"—she looked into her tub of ice cream—"and melting in this tub. So, unless you think I *need* a lawyer, please get the hell out of my house."

"You shouldn't talk to your fans like that, Queen Hynata. We're just doing our jobs. Marcel is doing his. We're doing ours."

"And yours is . . . Oh, never mind, Marcel. I don't want to know. But for you, Mr. Fan Club President, just so you know, I'm not the queen anymore. I quit my job today."

"Lacy—" Marcel began.

"Yes, I had a little accident a few months back and it's causing me some problems that are gonna take time to fix," Lacy said, sounding somewhat saddened. "So you can take your fan club and get the fuck out . . . Okay?" Lacy said to Jim, who just smirked.

Lawrence, on the other hand, smiled at her. "Thank you for your cooperation and we will check your alibi, okay?"

Lacy nodded as if no more words would come.

Aretha walked past the two of them in the doorway and paused. "We'll be in the car, Marcel," she said, sounding sad.

"Okay," he told her. "Lacy," he began, turning back to her.

"I can't believe you did this to me! Have you been watching me? Is that your job? Is that why you went to your parents'? Oh my God! You fucked me, Marcel . . . in more ways than one!"

"Lacy!" Marcel was shocked at how vicious she was sounding. He'd never seen Lacy this angry before. She was beyond the woman he recognized. She was sounding more and more like the cartoon character she portrayed on television.

"Oops," she said, repeating his own tone used before making love to her that morning in her bed. She slammed the door.

Chapter 55

The ride back to town was quiet for Aretha and Marcel, who rode in the back seat of Jim and Lawrence's car.

"So that's your girlfriend, eh, Celly?" Jim said teasingly.

"No, and I'm not going to tell you guys that again."

"Well good, because she's pregnant," Jim said.

Marcel sat forward. "What?"

"Baby books and shit all over the place," Jim went on.

Marcel looked at Aretha, who now looked totally disgusted with Jim and his blabbering. "Thanks, Jim. God, people do like handling their shit their way sometimes!" Aretha barked.

"You knew?" Marcel asked her. Aretha turned to him.

"I knew the first time I saw her she was pregnant. I just didn't know if the baby was yours. I mean, you keep acting like y'all ain't kicking it."

"We aren't. I mean, we . . ."

"Is the baby yours or not?" Lawrence asked.

"How the hell do I know?" Marcel blurted.

"You know. If she's the one for you, Celly—you'll know," Jim said, sounding almost like an adult.

"Wow. What do I do? She hates me now. I mean, I just accused her of murder."

"No, you didn't. You did your job. She's gonna respect you for that. Go back over there and make it right with her."

"No. Not yet. I have to get to the bottom of all this first. I have to—"

"We know, Marcel. You're a good cop. But if she's pregnant with your kid, then you have a responsibility that goes beyond being a cop," Lawrence added.

"Besides, how you gonna find out if it's your kid without talking to her?" Aretha asked.

Marcel sat quietly for a moment and then pulled out his cell phone. "Hello, Denise."

Chapter 56

Marcel touched Charla's back. She turned over quickly, showing that she had not been asleep. "Charla, we need to talk."

"About what?"

"Us."

Instantly Charla sat up in the bed. It was almost as if she anticipated this conversation. Marcel wasn't sure whether she looked forward to it or dreaded it. Either way it needed to be had. He'd found out from Denise that indeed Lacy was pregnant and that it was his baby—according to her. Lacy wouldn't lie about a thing like that. It wasn't as if she intended to trap him. It wasn't as if she intended for any of this to happen. She was just as caught up in this as he was.

"Marcel," Charla called, bringing him back to the conversation.

"I don't even know where to begin."

"Try the beginning."

"Okay, well . . . Ever just want to be attached to somebody?"

"You mean like in handcuffs." Charla chuckled slightly.

"No, like emotionally."

Charla looked around. "Where is this coming from, Marcel? You feeling old or something? No, I told you, I don't want to meet your folks. I don't want to get married. I want it to stay the way it is."

"But what if I want more?"

"Marcel—if you want more, then I say go get more."

Stunned, Marcel stared at Charla for a long time. "You mean, you're not even gonna try to save this? Charla, I thought what we had was big—huge."

"No, you didn't." Charla chuckled. "If you did, you would have stopped loving Lacy Durham."

"What?"

"You've always loved her. You watch her cartoon, for crying out loud. You didn't think I knew that? You don't think I watch your face while you listen to the voice of that damned Queen Hynata?"

"I . . . I don't know what to say. I don't know what we're supposed to do right at this moment."

"Tell me the truth. You sleeping with her?"

Marcel hesitated. At that Charla grabbed her pillow and threw herself onto her side. "Then there ya go. That's what we do. It's over. I'm moving out. You're moving on. It's that easy."

"Charla." Marcel touched her shoulder only to have her grab his hand in a painful grip without looking at him.

"I've been as nice as I'm going to ever be about this, Marcel. I have to work tonight and I need to get some sleep. When I wake up—be gone. Stay gone until after I come in tomorrow and get my shit. Then don't ever, ever try to talk to me again. Okay?"

Marcel was gripped with pain but managed to nod. "Okay. Yeah." He pulled his hand free from her loosened grip. All he could think about was Queen Hynata and how well Charla could play that role right now.

Chapter 57

"You're insane. You are totally out of control."

"And you're having a marvelous time being served and probably"—Sonja looked over the nurse's backside as she left the room—"serviced by a bunch of fuckin' nurses who think you're the shit. You telling them all about your plans to live the cushy life of a millionaire."

"What are you talking about? Adam is dead."

"Why are you telling me? Phoebe is the one behind all this shit. She is the one out of control. I'm the one helping you out. Oh, that wasn't part of the fuckin' plan either?" Sonja vented through gritted teeth. "I told you if we didn't stick to the original plan, people were gonna get hurt." Sonja flailed her arms after taking a long-throated drink from the flask she pulled from her purse and then tossing it roughly back inside. "So, now what, you planning to get out and maybe hook up with her?"

"With her? Who in God's name are you talking about?"

"Don't play me stupid. I knew as soon as I told you Phoebe was still alive you'd try to hook up with her."

"Sonja, I never would have known she was really alive until you told me. I really thought I was dreaming that she was coming to my bed."

"Save me." Sonja balked, looking again to her purse for some relief.

"I didn't know, I really didn't know. So did you really kill him?"

"You fool! I didn't kill him. Phoebe did it. She killed Victoria too. Don't you see?"

"No, I don't."

"And I don't give a fuck. Either way, the money is as good as yours . . . ours." She started speaking in French. She was such a chameleon. She began rubbing on Harold's chest and then farther down. He caught her hand.

"Don't start playing games with my mind. I know you killed them . . . both of them," Harold growled in a low tone. Sonja flung her hair over her shoulder and slowly raised his gown, exposing his manhood. "So don't start playing the Euro diva with me. I know how you get when you're angry. I mean, my God, you flew across the Atlantic just to come slap my face, so you don't think I believe that you killed Adam?"

Sonja stroked Harold's cheek with a hard, passion-filled swipe that was almost a slap. "And what a pretty face it is. Does she kiss your face?" Sonja said, pulling Harold by the cheeks into a full-mouth kiss.

"Stop it. You've become nothing more than a jealous bitch. You don't even know what you're doing anymore. With Adam dead, I will be expected to get another attorney and that attorney is going to play by the rules."

"And then what? You'll get the money and then what? You act like you aren't entitled to the money. The only reason we had a problem was because Adam was greedy. He wanted a cut. Now with him out of the picture it's just me and you. Fuck Phoebe. I think she's in hiding anyway. She won't come out."

"How can you be sure?"

"She thinks she killed . . ." Sonja stopped speaking. "Trust me, she just won't come out."

"Thinks she killed somebody? So she didn't kill anybody just like I thought. You did it. You are insane,

Sonja. I'm going to tell what you've done," Harold said, stupidly reaching for the phone. Sonja's grip tightened on his penis. He froze.

"Don't go. Please don't go back to her. I know you have a soft spot for Phoebe and maybe even that red-headed bitch . . ." Sonja paused as if hearing her own words. "God, I hate redheads . . . But you can't do this to me."

"Why did you kill him? Adam was on our side. Even before I knew Phoebe was alive I trusted that Adam was on our side."

Sonja looked away. "Why did you turn on him then? You see, Harold, I was helping you narrow down things. You say Adam was on your side, yet you were ready to double cross him the moment I told you Phoebe was alive. You were ready to double cross us all."

Sonja began looking at the IVs and other tubes hooked up to Harold. "So they are cleaning you out, eh?" She abruptly changed the subject. Harold watched her closely. She moved around the room like a serpent. "I could kill you right now," she said. "But you're my only link to the money."

"But what if I don't get it? What if they find a reason to give it to Lacy?"

"They won't, because Lacy will be dead."

Harold suddenly felt a chill. He hugged himself, rubbing his arms up and down. "My head is spinning. I need to eat something. I should call the nurse."

"Harold, I warn you, if you say anything, you'll go to jail for killing Victoria."

"Sonja," Harold began.

"If you say anything . . ." she threatened. "Now, sweetheart, I'll be back later. I have a couple of things to do in preparation for you coming home."

"You're not going to be able to prove Lacy killed Adam or Victoria."

"Watch me. . . ."

At that Sonja blew him a kiss and left the room. Harold knew then that Sonja was crazy. He reached for the phone and called Marcel at work, but he didn't answer at his desk.

Chapter 58

"How come I'm just finding this out?" Marcel yelped upon hearing the news about Steven Prophet.

"Why would anybody think to call you? The man had a family. They thought he was gonna die; calling you wasn't on their list of things to do," Aretha explained.

"Okay, so two weeks ago, Steven Prophet was brought in with internal bleeding . . . et cetera, et cetera . . . He goes into shock during surgery; ends up in a coma. Okay, now what?"

"Now he's awake and the first person he asks for is you," Aretha said as they parked in the hospital parking lot. "Go figure."

"Wow," Marcel said. "This is craziness."

They entered the floor where Steven was. He lay in bed with his daughter holding his hand. "Sweetie, go out with the nice lady for a moment and let me talk with the policeman, okay?"

"Okay, Daddy," she said, smiling at Marcel and moving over to Aretha. "I know you're not in trouble because you've been asleep."

Steven and Marcel waited to start speaking until the door closed behind the little girl and Aretha.

"Wow, I had no idea you were in here. I got so caught up in work and trying to figure out who did what, I didn't even think that you could be in the middle of it all."

"No worries. I had a good nap," Steven joked.

"What happened, Steven?"

"You tell me."

"Victoria Stillberg and Adam Stillberg are both dead."

Steven flinched.

"I just found out today about this. Apparently, you were found on the steps of a house that belonged to Adam Stillberg. You were hit with the same bat used to kill Barry Nugent."

Steven flinched again. "Nugent is dead too, eh?"

"Yeah. Do you remember why you were there? Do you remember?"

"Yes. I do. I had followed a woman there. I had decided to play P.I. and I went to Harold Kitchener's apartment. I saw a redheaded woman leave. I thought it might be Lacy Durham so I followed her. She didn't go to the house I knew to be hers, she went into Pacifica. I got to the house, knocked on the door. When she opened the door, I took a picture and then . . ."

"Then?"

"Things get real fuzzy after that."

"Who was the woman?" Marcel asked.

"The woman?"

"When you took the picture of the woman, who was it?"

"Hell, you tell me. This woman had dark hair and brown eyes, but, then again, so did Marilyn this time."

"Marilyn?"

Steven rose up a bit as if making sure the door was really closed. "Yeah, my fantasy girl. I saw her at Adam's office. She was a woman who looked like Marilyn Monroe. She was blond with these perfect pouty lips and a body that was like . . . wow. She looked like an angel. That's when I thought I was gonna die, because right before I went out, that devil woman disappeared and my Marilyn angel came. I think she's the one who called the ambulance. You may want to check that 911 call."

"Could you identify either woman if you saw either one again?"

"Well, yeah. You show me a picture of Marilyn and I'll show you . . ."

At that Marcel pulled out a picture of Phoebe dressed up for a school play—*Diamonds Are a Girl's Best Friend*. She played Marilyn Monroe.

Steven's eyes widened. "Oh my God, that's her."

"Are you positive?"

"Yes. I'd know that angel anywhere."

"That's my sister, Steven. That's Phoebe."

"Get outta here!"

"Are you telling me my sister is alive?"

Steven looked at Marcel intensely. "If your sister is alive, this case meant nothing. If your sister is alive, people died for nothing."

"What does it mean for Lacy?"

"Same as it means for Harold—it's a fraudulent case. We start looking to see who committed the fraud—the porn maker or the manslayer," Steven said. Marcel stared at him, looking for an indication of how he planned to proceed.

"I don't think Lacy did anything fraudulent. Plus she . . ." Marcel grew quiet but his face warmed up a bit. "She has an alibi for all of the murders."

"Interesting, and very convenient too." Steven smiled. "How long have you two been together?"

"We're not together. We're friends. We're . . ."

"No need to explain."

"Good, because I can't. All I know is that for some reason my sister wanted her to have a million dollars . . . a million dollars that four people have died trying to keep her from getting."

"Do you think your sister is alive?"

Marcel thought long and hard before answering. "Do you?"

Steven looked at the picture again. "Let me tell you this. While I was out, I had a dream. They say when you're in a coma you hear people talking to you but you just can't answer them. I guess they're right because while I was out, Marilyn was talking to me." Steven smiled. "She told me she was sorry about all this. She told me some horrible things that her husband had made her do for money. She said at first it was okay; she felt small and insignificant. She said she wasn't the girl everybody thought she was in school. She said that she was ready for life to change. She said that she wanted to die and move forward—strange combination, I thought."

Marcel listened and then sat quietly soaking in Steven's words. "And she did, you know. I mean, even if she like . . ." Marcel hesitated. "She died to everyone who loved her—she's gone, Steven."

"Okay, then let your captain close the case. End this. Stop looking for her."

"If I end this the way it is right now, Harold will get the money, and this is all about the money with him. He murdered my sister and—"

"It usually is about money, Marcel. You can't change that. You can't change anything. You can only move forward. By the way, how is Ms. Durham?"

"She's fine—oblivious to all this."

"Thanks to you?"

Marcel smiled. "Probably."

Steven now grew serious. "Marcel, I'm sorry I couldn't help you any more than I did. That whole night was so fuzzy. I go to catch a crook and end up nearly getting myself killed. How do you do this every day of your life?"

"I just don't think about it that hard, I guess."

"I'm an insurance investigator. I'm normally behind the desk. The first time I really got into my job I nearly lost my life. I was nearly taken away from my little girl. I will never risk my life like that again."

"Every day is a risk, Steven."

"Yeah, I guess. But this one took me where I never want to go again."

"Yeah, I understand. This case has taken a lot of people where they didn't need to go," Marcel said, thinking of him and Lacy and what he was going to need to fix. "I lost my sister."

"But, if I'm not wrong . . . you gained something, too."

Marcel smiled. "I don't know what you mean."

"Every time I say Ms. Durham's name you get all goofy."

Marcel turned away slightly. "Yeah, well."

"So I'm saying if people are really dying trying to get that stinking money away from her, then I say let Harold Kitchener have it—draw the missiles in his direction. I will tell you, though, if it comes out that Harold had anything to do with any of this, he'll lose the money and it will go to Lacy and . . ."

"I'll lose my badge protecting Lacy from whoever tries to hurt her."

"Make it easy. Stay close to her and watch over her, and catch the son of a bitch who took your sister's life away."

"Can you tell me anything else?"

"Well, the more I think about that night, the more I think I remember hearing another name—Sonja. Does that make any sense to you?"

Chapter 59

Lacy called her boss, lied and begged and finally in the end got the rest of the month off. She'd been home for about three days now. They'd rerun the show and/or fire her if they needed to. Even the pets seemed to notice that she was home more. It was almost as if her being there was cramping their style. They would begin to roughhouse through the living room and notice her on the sofa and freeze. It made her wonder what they did when she wasn't there.

She'd be going to her parents' soon and just figured she might even house hunt in the old neighborhood. "Why not? My mom would love having me there. I could play cards with her and the 'gang' on Friday nights," she mumbled. Mrs. DuChamp would get to see her grandkids and not even know about it, she thought, feeling good about the possibilities. Besides, she got a letter just that afternoon telling her she would be receiving the insurance money as beneficiary of Phoebe Kitchener's double indemnity policy.

She tried not to think about Harold and the part he played in Phoebe's death. She didn't want to think about anything but what Dave had told her about the insurance money—and he was right. There was no way that kind of money would come trouble free. "That's so funny that I told Dave about the money. I do not remember telling him anything about the insurance or the money. . . ."

Ending up at Dave's place, she hesitated to intrude, but she finally just accepted that if things were ever going to be normal in life she had to start now trying to make that happen. Just then she saw Raven out on the deck. She was looking over Dave's plants. The rains had eased up but they had left a mess where his beautiful botanical garden used to be.

"Yuck," she heard her groan.

Lacy eased up on the deck. She cleared her throat so as not to alarm her. Raven turned to her. Her blue eyes were the color of the ocean. Her hair was a dyed blond but still a good color for her complexion, which looked naturally tanned.

"Hi, I'm—"

Raven outstretched her hand. "Lacy Durham. I know."

"How? Oh yeah." Lacy slapped her forehead. "Dave must have told you."

"You seem jumpy."

"I'm sorry. I've just got so much on my mind," Lacy said, running her fingers through her hair. When she did that her jacket opened, exposing her baby bulge, which was getting harder to hide. Raven's eyes locked on it.

"Are you pregnant?" she asked bluntly.

Lacy drew her jacket around her. The moment between them drew tense. "Uh . . . yes. Yes, I am—twins."

Raven's eyes lit up. "Twins! My God, how exciting. Come sit. Tell me how you feel."

Raven quickly pulled up two lawn chairs. She ran inside and retrieved the teapot. She'd made some jasmine tea. Lacy could smell it. "I'll make you a cup. It's got no caffeine; of course, I ruin that with my sweet tooth," she rambled, putting teaspoon after teaspoon of sugar in her cup.

Lacy's heart tightened. She'd only known two other people on earth to add that much sugar to their beverages. "My best friend used to drink her tea like that."

Raven froze. She handed Lacy an unsweetened cup. "Your *best* friend?"

"Yes. I didn't realize she was my best friend until she died. It's crazy how we do that."

"Yes," Raven said, sipping her tea. "Sometimes we don't realize many things until we die," she said.

The comment was odd, and Lacy wondered what she meant. "Pardon?"

"Oh, nothing. I was just thinking out loud. Tell me about your babies. I would love to have a baby but . . . I can't."

"I'm sorry to hear that. Well, if I stay on this hill there will be plenty of babies for all of us." Lacy laughed.

"And the father?" she finally asked after a couple more sips.

Lacy's face dropped slightly. "He's not involved. This wasn't planned."

"Ahh, I heard you call me accident prone, once. It appears we both might be."

"Oh God, I'm sorry. That was so rude of me," Lacy said, feeling the heat rising.

Raven smiled. When she did, Lacy was drawn into it. She stared deep into the woman's eyes, which now seemed unnatural in color. Everything about her now seemed unnatural and misplaced. It was as if she wore a mask over the real her. Lacy wanted to touch her face to see if perhaps it was plastic, but she refrained. "I love him, don't get me wrong," she confessed.

"I know you do," Raven answered.

"You do?"

"You're a successful woman. I doubt that a baby, let alone twins, really fit into your life right now. You'd have to love the man to even attempt this sacrifice."

"I hadn't thought about that way, but . . ." Lacy smiled. "Perhaps."

"Then I take it all back. Love is never an accident."

Chapter 60

Marcel entered Harold's office. He reached for the phone. "Security."

"Wait! Put the damn phone down, Harold. I'm not here to kick your ass."

He hesitated but then hung up.

"How's Sonja?"

"Wouldn't know. She's in France."

"Don't try to blow smoke up my ass. She's right here in the city. She's been here for a long time. She's the star in a couple of your movies—Harold."

"Movies?" Harold shifted uneasily.

"Yeah, the movies you make in your condo and on . . . boats."

"Boats?"

"The movie you and Phoebe and Adam and Sonja were making the night that boat blew up and my sister . . . disappeared. I thought it was interesting that you weren't there. Where were you, Harold?"

"Where?"

"Where were you?"

"I was . . . um . . . busy."

"Busy with Sonja? Busy with Adam?"

"Just busy."

"You knew all along Phoebe was going to try to kill you on that boat, huh?"

"No! Not until Sonja told me. I mean . . ." He paused. "I knew something was fishy, but I didn't know Phoebe was trying to kill me."

"You also didn't know she hadn't left you the money, huh?"

Harold stared at Marcel. The look was of pure ignorance and innocence. Harold was a bumbler. He had played all his cards to see where they landed. He was as ignorant and innocent as Lacy—sort of. Lacy had her hand in none of it and ended up in the middle of it—without knowing what was going on. Harold, on the other hand, had his hand in all of it and still didn't have a clue which side he should be on. "It's all about the money to you, right, Harold?"

"Maybe. What's your point? Because no matter what any of it is about, I nearly died. Victoria did die. She was a sweet woman."

"I agree. Don't you want to get who killed her?"

"I know who killed her." Harold leaned in close. "Phoebe did it?"

"You know as well as I do Phoebe didn't kill anybody. She doesn't have the heart."

"She sure as hell has the heart to kill me!"

"Well you pissed her off, but other people, no. I don't think she has it in her to kill like that."

"So what are you saying?"

"I'm saying you keep hiding Sonja and you're going to go to jail for all of it. You're gonna take the blame for all of it. Work with us here and we'll help you."

"Us? I don't see an *us*. I see a *you* and you hate my guts."

"But I love . . . I loved my sister more."

Chapter 61

Harold was livid. Lacy had won the case and was going to be granted the money. Not only was he now out of a million dollars, he was being investigated for murder. Somehow, following an anonymous call, a baseball bat and camera were found in his garage. Forensics found hair remains of both Barry Nugent and Steven Prophet on the bat. Additionally, a note written in Phoebe's hand was found, indicating that she feared for her life. The letter stated that she worried that her husband was trying to kill her because of his affair with Sonja Farrar. That led to Sonja being questioned as well as detained in the country until investigations were completed. Harold yelled and screamed at his attorney for his inability to get him out of these jams he was finding himself in—daily. His new attorney had no response except to remind him of the law—and that he followed it by the letter. It was all a bit too perfect as far as Harold was concerned.

"You know Phoebe is trying to screw us both," Sonja barked.

"Oh, please, they said that letter was written prior to her death."

"And her brother is a cop. Give me a fuckin' break. You act like he's so honest. He's as crooked as . . . as your dick," she said before bursting into laughter.

"Sonja, get serious. I'm being tied into a murder investigation, Sonja! My company is now being investigated for illegal activities as well."

"Well you shouldn't have paid your secretary to have sex with you!" Sonja yelped.

"I didn't."

"That's not how the courts see it!"

"I'm ruined."

"Oh, quit whining. Phoebe is gonna come out of hiding the minute Lacy gets that check and I'm telling you, I'm ready for that bitch. She'll really be dead when I get through with her."

"What are you gonna do?"

"If I tell you—you'll be an accessory to the fact."

"What do I have to lose? If I lose. Which I won't, right?"

"Look at you . . . getting all murderous on me," Sonja joked. "It makes me hot."

"You really are a sick little girl."

"Yes, I am."

"Tell me, how do you plan to get the money after you kill Lacy Durham?"

"Please, if I tell you, I may have to kill you too."

"Tell me. I love living on the edge," he teased.

Sonja wasn't stupid, or at least she didn't feel she was. Harold was too eager to get involved in her little plan. She was suspicious by nature and now Harold had her doubting.

"I'm going to kill Lacy. I'm going to shoot her at her own house. No, better yet—you're going to."

"Why?"

"Because . . . she killed Phoebe."

"Ahhh . . . When?"

"Don't be so eager. I'll tell you when you need to know."

"But how is that going to look like an accident?"

"Please." Sonja smacked her lips. "I'm horny now," she said, reaching for the anal oil.

Chapter 62

Lacy's mind drifted off earth and on to other places of interest. Marcel. She'd not heard from him in a long time. Okay, so it had only been a couple of weeks, but still. She missed him like crazy.

She'd not written anything for a minute and figured eventually her muse would come to her. Maybe living in a more familiar environment would help. *You can't just expect her to drop in on ya; you have to get things ready and conducive,* Lacy told herself. *She's not like Raven, dropping from the sky—perfect and all that.*

Perfection.

Just the word made her see Marcel's face.

Suddenly the house phone rang. Lacy looked at the clock. It was just about eleven P.M. She hesitated answering it but slowly picked up the receiver. "Hello?"

"Hi," Marcel said.

Her heart leapt. "Hi," she answered.

"What are you doing?" he asked.

She looked around at the dogs lounging in front of her space heater. They seemed to be getting use to the comotions that were apart of her household. She glanced at her workspace covered with unfinished things. "Working," she lied.

"Really?" he asked. "You're not lounging and being a queen?" he joked.

She giggled uncontrollably. Marcel did that to her. She felt stupid and girlish. "No. I'm really busy. Besides, I told you I quit that job and I'm working hard on something else now," she lied.

"Well, then, maybe I should let you go," he said.

"Uh, no," she quickly said, jumping to her feet and smoothing down her baggy sweats. "I mean, yeah, maybe so—you were right, there's no sense in trying to make something where there isn't anything." She winced at her words. She never wanted Marcel to let her go. But in her heart she knew it was best. He had someone and that someone wasn't her. This call was . . . She didn't know what it was, but she couldn't make more of it than whatever it was. She couldn't get carried away. *Oh my gosh, his voice is so wonderful,* she thought. A sigh escaped her lips. "Besides, I'm a millionaire now and you're just so out of my league." She chuckled. "You know, I wonder how many people know who I didn't tell. I was just realizing even my neighbor knew about it. Maybe I told him. I don't know."

"You don't know if you told him? You tell him everything."

"No. I never told him about us. But, then again, there wasn't anything to tell," she said, rubbing her rounding belly. "I've just been feeling crazy, I guess. Harold's not the only one feeling and doing insane things. I mean, since Phoebe died nothing has been the same in the world."

"You have a neighbor who knew about your insurance money and you didn't tell him—first of all, you have a neighbor. Where does he live? I never saw any other houses up there."

Lacy smacked her lips. That was Marcel, never wanting to address the serious things in life. *Maybe he is just jealous,* Lacy hoped. "Yes, Marcel, and he's my friend," she said with a chuckle, leaving out the fact that friends were all she and Dave would ever be— maybe even more like family. Raven too was an immediate friend. There was something about her that Lacy was just drawn to and it seemed very mutual. Yes, she needed to see her parents and make some decisions about life.

She was so torn on what to do now.

Marcel watched her though the large bay window, pacing the floor as she spoke to him. She had no idea he watched her. He felt voyeuristic. On this hill with no one around for nearly a mile, anyone could be out here, but instead no one was. Tonight it was just he and Lacy on the top of the world . . . alone.

"I'm glad you're not angry," he said.

"No. I'm not angry. I just think we shouldn't talk," she said.

He saw her wipe her face with the back of her hand. Was she crying? His heart melted. He wanted to go right through that window and take her in his arms. He wanted to tell her he loved her. But he couldn't. Why?

"I'm a dick," he admitted to her. "I'm a dick with no balls," he added.

"No. You're not."

"I should not have said what I said to you or let what happened happen. I mean—"

"It's okay. It happens. I mean, I'm just glad you didn't screw up your life with . . . with Charla."

"Yeah." Marcel felt sick. He'd more than screwed up his life with Charla.

When Marcel met Charla a couple of years back, it was easy to fall for her. She was strong and detached. She was cool. On Fridays after work she would be at the pub with the rest of the gang, chugging brews and swearing like a sailor. When he told his jokes, she laughed. They had a mutual physical attraction and that was enough for then. Charla didn't even want to meet his parents, which he thought was in the rule-book. "Naw, I don't want to meet them," was all she had said. Marcel liked that in a woman, to the point and without strings attached, at least at the time.

No one *got him* like Charla did, no one except Lacy, and to think of it, Charla got him as a cop. Lacy got him and got *to* him. She got to his heart.

Why hadn't he seen that earlier in life? Why? Phoebe had told him that Lacy was living with some guy up on a hill—*in paradise.* Phoebe had told him that she was happy and very attached. It wasn't like him to home wreck, and besides, she'd not acted as if there was anything there. She never showed him how she felt—either that or he was just too much of a jackass to see. More than likely the latter, he realized now, watching her through the window. He could almost feel her loneliness.

And he knew loneliness. He could spot it a mile away. Hell, he saw it every morning in the mirror. "Look. I'ma let you go, okay?" he said to Lacy now.

"Okay," she responded. Her voice was soft and breathy. Marcel watched as Lacy hung up the phone before she pulled her big robe around her and cuddled up in the blanket they had shared that cold morning after the funeral. She just sat there for nearly an hour—crying. Until she finally drifted off to sleep.

Curiosity got the best of Marcel. He wasn't one to let new information slip through his fingers. He drove for what was about a half mile before he saw lights coming from a small bungalow down near the cliffs. The road leading to it was narrow and surely he'd need his lights to get closer to the house. He wanted to see, however, so he got out of his car with his flashlight and gun in hand. Lacy had never spoken about any wildlife being up here, *and with her scaredy-cat ass surely she would have told me something,* he thought while heading down the rugged, narrow road leading to the house.

He reached the house. It was dark except for a couple of lights. One was outside and the other one was a small one that hovered over a large painting. Marcel stared at the portrait. It was a nude painting of a raven-haired beauty with dark, soulful eyes. Staring at the woman he nearly lost his breath, for in the painting he saw Phoebe—in all her beautiful glory. "How did he get this?" Marcel's voice came in a whisper. "How is it possible? Could Harold be telling the truth?

Just then he heard noise from inside the house. He ducked in the heavy shrubs. Inside he saw the blond woman. She was laughing and carrying on with a man—that neighbor, no doubt. It hadn't taken too much research for Marcel to learn his name. Dave. Yes, this was probably him, Marcel deduced. He stared at her from all the angles as they danced and played like young lovers. Her profile was familiar, yet when she turned face on, her nose wasn't right. Her lips were narrow and thin—Phoebe's were pouty and full. The woman's eyes were blue—dancing blue. They danced the dance that Phoebe's eyes knew but with the wrong color dictating their steps. In a way, the woman's face looked fake—created by a surgeon's knife instead of nature. *Marcel, you're making this up,* he told himself. *You're making all of this up. Phoebe died. The painting. The woman. The fact that Harold swore that Phoebe is still alive. What if . . .*

The man took the woman in his arms and kissed her tenderly—lovingly. The woman smiled. So rich and sincere was her grin, Marcel realized then that she could not be Phoebe. Phoebe had never smiled like that. She would have never taken love from a man like Dave. He was old and clearly ordinary. Phoebe liked the bright lights and the pretty people. That was her problem with Lacy—she loved Lacy but couldn't get over the fact that Lacy lived on earth—and she, in the clouds.

And perhaps that's where you are now, Marcel thought, shaking his head free of the crazy thoughts. He marched back up the hill to his car.

Chapter 63

For the first time since moving into the house Lacy had a dinner party. She invited Denise and her husband, and Dave and Raven. Of course, Denise wondered why Marcel had been kept out of the loop, but Lacy just ignored the comment.

"Let's toast to accidental friends and purposeful relationships," Dave said, holding up his glass and kissing Raven before taking a sip.

Lacy giggled before sipping her champagne. Her doctor had told her it would be fine for her to have a little.

"Oh my gosh!" Raven exclaimed. "The gift. We forgot the gift!"

"Oh poo. I'll go get it," Dave agreed.

"Are you sure?" Raven said, kissing his cheek.

Lacy balked. "Oh, yuck, if you guys kiss one more time, I'ma puke."

Denise laughed. "You know you wanna kissy face with Marcel right now."

"Marcel kissy facing. I can't see that," Raven said, clearly caught up in the moment.

Lacy caught it. "What do you mean by that?"

"Tell you what. You come with me!" Dave suggested, tugging at Raven's sleeve.

"Yes," she quickly agreed, setting down her drink and rushing out.

Denise waited until they had cleared the path toward Dave's place before she spoke. "She's freaking me out."

"Don't start, Denise. Yes, I have to say Raven is a bit different but—"

"But nothing. She's freaking me the hell out! That's not the first little faux pas she made tonight."

"Stop looking for them and you'll stop finding them."

"Whatever you say, Ms. Millionaire."

The three of them laughed.

Lacy felt happy. She felt happy enough for the situation she was in. She'd gotten her check, and despite her mother's warning of it being only $75,000, it was far more than that. She'd even given her parents $75,000 and it didn't make a dent. Eugene was helping her invest the money wisely as he was good at his job. In just a week, he'd earned her $3,000 dollars on her investments. "When you invest big, you get big returns," he told her.

Just then, there was a knock at the door. Lacy thought it was Dave being formal. She opened it to find Harold and Sonja there. "Party and we weren't invited?" Sonja said, sauntering in.

"What do you want? This is a private party," Lacy said firmly.

Sonja looked down at her belly. "You're fuckin' knocked up? Who's the daddy? This stud right here?" she asked of Eugene.

Denise stepped forward. "Hell no. You know this is my husband!"

"Oh yeah, I'd forgotten. I can't keep track of everybody's shit like you do." Sonja pushed past Lacy. Lacy gave Harold a stare. She could have sworn she saw him wink. But she was livid and not really looking for signs of any kind. "How does it feel to be living off Harold's money?"

"It's not Harold's money. Phoebe left it to me and under the circumstances I need it now."

"Yeah, I'm sure she'd be thrilled to know you were using it to pay for a baby. Considering—"

"You're a bitch, you know that?"

"Look, you killed Phoebe and now I'ma kill you!" Harold blurted awkwardly.

"I knew you would do this!" Denise blurted.

Lacy looked at her as if she was crazy. "You did?" Lacy asked.

"That's too bad, Denise, your Ms. Know-it-all-ness finally got you in over your head!" Harold answered.

"Denise, what does he mean?" Lacy asked.

"I don't really know. I was just talking. . . ." Denise said, hiding behind Eugene.

"She's a damn know-it-all . . . always has been. She has been in everybody's mix . . . Worse than a damn P.I."

"Baby, are they telling the truth? You knew about this stuff?"

"No. I mean, yes. I mean, I knew Sonja was up to no good. I've been following her. I knew she and Phoebe were plotting something. That's why I tried to warn you so many times to get Marcel up here—"

"Phoebe?" Lacy blurted. "Phoebe is dead!"

Sonja came from Lacy's kitchen with Lacy's gun. "My God you are a creature of habit. Phoebe told me you kept it in your kitchen drawer. I would never have believed her." Aiming the gun she shot at Harold, grazing him.

Denise and Lacy screamed. Even Eugene jumped slightly.

"Shit, Sonja!" Harold yelped.

"And now you're dead too. Shoot her, Harold. We have witnesses that she admitted to killing Phoebe.

That you got into it and Harold shot you. By morning a wire transfer into Phoebe's overseas account will clean out your bank account. I have access to that account, so bye-bye, Ms. Millionaire."

Harold fired the gun over Lacy's head. She screamed and ducked. About that time the door burst open and Raven entered. "Sonja!" she screamed. "I knew you'd try something, you stupid bitch!"

"Phoebe!" Sonja screeched, charging at her. They began to wrestle, knocking over Lacy's pretty glasses. They crashed to the floor.

Lacy was speechless. She stood with her hands over her belly in protective mode, watching the unbelievable, while Denise ran to the phone to call the police. Harold dropped the gun and collapsed onto the sofa, moaning at his flesh wound. Lacy's gun went off for the second time since she bought it.

Dave and Marcel burst in. Marcel fired immediately; Sonja took the first bullet in the arm and then the second in the thigh. She fell away from the bleeding woman everyone knew only as Raven.

Epilogue

The thunder clapped. The waves crashed loudly against the rocks. The weather girl was right on the money today. Lacy laughed at the thought of her. Inside, however, Lacy felt calm with the loud booms and flashes of light outside her large bay window. It was amazing how a lifetime fear could just go away like that.

It had been a year since Phoebe died but life had moved on. Lacy had the twins. She named them Jourdan and Journey. They were two beautiful dark-eyed girls with pouty lips and deep, rich skin tones—and red hair.

Marcel stirred the fire before jumping back on the sofa next to her and under the throw that her mother made. Dave entered the living room with a tray of cheese puffs hot out of the oven. The smell was wonderful. "Oh my God," everyone groaned in ecstasy.

"Newest recipe, I'm adding it to the book," he said before sitting next to his beautiful wife. Lacy smiled at the woman who hugged one of her baby girls tight while singing a song she said she knew as a child. It was one her own mother had sung to her. It was one Marcel knew as well, and he eventually joined in.

"Raven hates these things," Dave admitted about his cheese puffs.

"No, I don't. I just don't want to get fat." She giggled after completing the verses to the lullaby and popping one in her mouth.

"You'll still be my perfect Raven angel," Dave said.

She ran her fingers through her thick blond hair. Her blue eyes danced in happiness. She was clearly filled with contentment. She smiled at Lacy with surgically constructed thin lips, her reconstructed nose wrinkling ever so slightly. Lacy smiled back.

Marcel wrapped his arms around Lacy's shoulders and kissed her cheek. No one said anything. Yet, out of reflex, everyone's eyes drifted above the mantel to the large painting of a dark-eyed beauty with raven-colored hair and pouty lips. The woman in the painting was dark and lonely. Dave hadn't intended to bring out those features; it just sort of happened accidentally. But Marcel had told him when he gave them the painting as a housewarming gift for their new home as a married couple that he'd portrayed his dead sister, Phoebe, perfectly.

The second twin joined Raven on her lap. They adored their Aunt Raven. After kissing the little girl that looked so much like Phoebe, short of the beautiful red curls, Raven broke into another song.

Again Marcel joined her, singing loudly.